BOOK 2
THE PEAKS SAGA

SEARCHING for MAIA

M.F. ERLER

SEARCHING FOR MAIA, Book 2
by M.F. Erler

Published by

WESTWIND PRESS
an imprint of First Steps Publishing
PO Box 571
Gleneden Beach, Oregon 97388-0571
FirstStepsPublishing.com

ISBN: 978-1-937333-67-6 (hb)
           978-1-937333-65-2 (pb)
           978-1-937333-66-9 (epub)

Bible quotes are from King James Version, and New International Version:
"Scripture taken from Holy Bible, New International Version (Registered Trademark) Copyright 1973,1978, 1984 by International Bible Society. Used by permission of Zondervan Publishing House. All rights reserved."

All lyrics quoted are Public Domain or composed by the author.

Cover illustration by Kabita Studios
Cover design, book formatting by Suzanne Fyhrie Parrott

Please provide feedback

10 9 8 7 6 5 4 3 2

Printed in U.S.A.

Praise for the Peaks Saga...

"I remember fondly reading The Lion, The Witch, and The Wardrobe *when I was in middle school.* The Peaks at the Edge of the World *has a similar mix of fantasy and adventure with a moral tale at its center. This is a book that's appropriate for a younger audience than most sci fi/fantasy novels. Enjoy the read!"*

—Kathy Dunhoff
ZOLA AWARD-WINNING WOMEN'S FICTION WRITER

"...a page turner!" *—Judith Seidel*

"Ms. Erler puts religion in new settings as she uses the characters in both the past and the future to meld the consequences of a religion lost, then found, then challenged. The ride is exciting. The characters real and engaging."

—Charlene Hecht
BA MUSIC EDUCATION
LONGTIME WRITER, INCLUDING "GUNSMOKE" FAN FICTION

"M.F. Erler skillfully pioneers a new writing genre, mixing elements of science fiction, dimensional time-travel, and modern Christian spirituality. She uses likeable characters in well-crafted settings in which we can identify with their real-life struggles."

—Richard Bartlett, MA, PhD

"...[M.F.] Erler's book, with its futuristic sci-fi focus and true-to-life grittiness, is not your typical Christian novel. At times, it unabashedly describes the realities of the darkness of humanity in order to contrast it with the power of hope and love found in God's grace. This unique book is well worth your time to read and I highly recommend it."

—Pastor Kevin Bueltmann
TRINITY LUTHERAN CHURCH - ASSOCIATE PASTOR
TRINITY LUTHERAN CAMP - EXECUTIVE DIRECTOR

Books by M.F. Erler

THE PEAKS SAGA

PEAKS AT THE EDGE OF THE WORLD
Finding the Light

SEARCHING FOR MAIA

MOUNTAINTOPS AND VALLEYS

WHEN THE WORLD GROWS COLD

THE FOUNTAIN AND THE DESERT

BEYOND THE WORLD

WHERE ALL WORLDS END

THIS BOOK IS DEDICATED TO
MY HUSBAND PAUL

Contents

THE PEAKS SAGA. 2

CHAPTER 1 ~ DUST IN THE WIND. 9

CHAPTER 2 ~ JON'S STORY BEGINS 17

CHAPTER 3 ~ DON'T PUSH THE RIVER. 36

CHAPTER 4 ~ THE SIGN AND THE RETURN 49

CHAPTER 5 ~ THE FAR EDGE OF NOWHERE. . . .59

CHAPTER 6 ~ THE FAR OUTPOST. 74

CHAPTER 7 ~ THE HEAVENS ARE TELLING 85

CHAPTER 8 ~ FATINA. .98

CHAPTER 9 ~ THE PASSIVE PLANET. 110

CHAPTER 10 ~ JOHAN AND THE BOOK 132

CHAPTER 11 ~ SEEK FIRST THE KINGDOM 164

CHAPTER 12 ~ FLIGHT FROM REASON. 171

CHAPTER 13 ~ SPECIAL KNOWLEDGE. 194

CHAPTER 14 ~ THE OPPOSING SIDE 221

CHAPTER 15 ~ IN REBEL HANDS 236

SNEAK PREVIEW: THE PEAKS SAGA, BOOK 3 ~
    "MOUNTAINTOPS AND VALLEYS". 257

ABOUT THE AUTHOR. 265

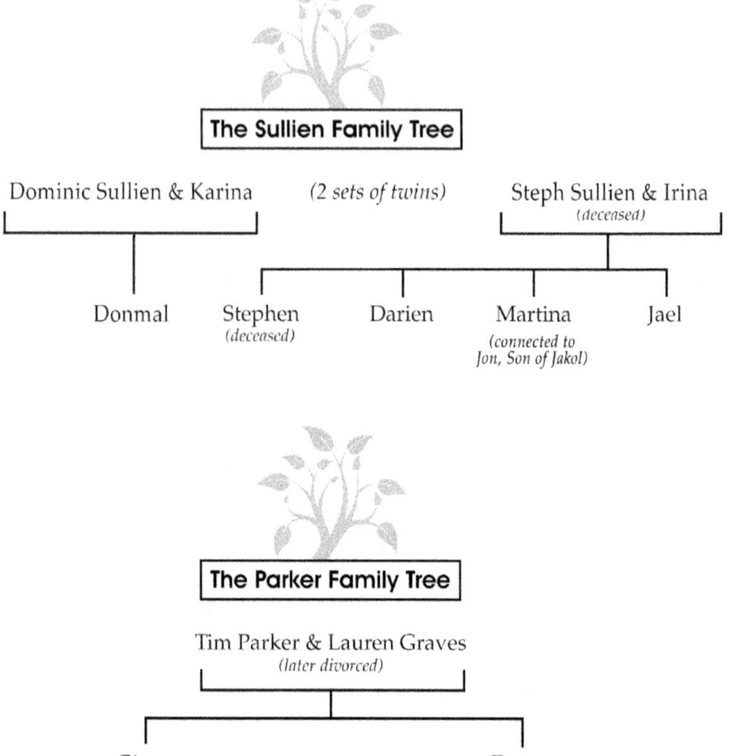

The Sullien Family Tree
Dominic Sullien & Karina
(2 sets of twins)
Steph Sullien & Irina
(deceased)
Donmal
Stephen
(deceased)
Darien
Martina
(connected to
Jon, Son of Jakol)
Jael
The Parker Family Tree
Tim Parker & Lauren Graves
(later divorced)
Ginna
(experimentally connected to Martina)
Danny
(experimentally connected to Jael)

CHAPTER 1

DUST IN THE WIND

Danny Parker stood at the window listening to the mournful howl of the wind. When was it ever going to stop? He felt their old house shudder with the strongest gusts. Looking down at the windowsill, he saw the layer of fine, black dust getting thicker. These old windows just couldn't keep it out.

'I'll have to clean this place again,' he sighed to himself. 'No one else will.'

His mother was still working long hours in her public relations job at the big nuclear power plant outside of town. 'You'd think with all the hours she puts in, we'd be able to afford a better house by now,' he mused. 'But Mom says it's still too hard to make ends meet, since Dad isn't sending the child support he was supposed to.' This made him angry, though he didn't want to feel this way about his father.

So, five years after they'd come to this small town in

eastern Colorado, they were still living in the little, rickety house that had been "only temporary."

The reverberations of a deep bass rhythm were rising from his sister Ginna's room. Every day after school, all she did was retreat into her room and play loud music. Now that she was almost out of high school, so many things had changed between them. They just didn't communicate like they used to. They'd been very close in grade school, but now they seemed to be drawing farther apart with each passing day.

Danny sighed and began tracing patterns in the dust on the windowsill. He felt a lump rising in his throat and tried desperately to swallow it. 'I'm too old to cry!' he told himself. 'I'm almost fourteen years old. I have to be the man of this house now that Dad is gone for good.'

Despite his efforts, tears were already trickling down his cheeks. Two of them dropped into the dust on the sill and spread into strange patterns. Looking down through tear-blurred eyes, he blinked at the picture he saw. His finger had drawn a jagged line like a range of mountains. The tear shapes looked like two figures walking toward him out of a haze.

Yes, that really happened once, though it was over four years ago now, and seemed like forever. Jon and Jael came to them out of time—what they called the GAP. Jael shared the story of his life with them, and they found hope and strength to face their trials in this new home. But now that seemed so long ago. The hope he and Ginna once felt seemed to have dried up and blown away, with the dust in the wind out here on the barren plains.

Suddenly a terribly strong gust shook the house. Afraid the window might blow in, Danny stepped back, covering his face with his arm. When he looked at the window again, two blond figures were standing there, gazing into his eyes.

"Ginna!" he cried. "They're back!"

His sister poked her head out her bedroom door. "Who's back?" she demanded. "What are you bugging me for?"

"Jon and Jael are here," he said, trying to keep his voice from wavering.

The two figures smiled at him and stepped aside to reveal a third figure standing just behind them. This one was a girl only slightly taller than Jael. Her dark brown hair hung long and straight to her shoulders, and her deep green eyes seemed to flash as she glanced over at Ginna, who'd just stepped out of her door.

"I'm Martina Sullien, Jael's sister," she said. "We came at your call, Daniel and Virginia."

"Don't call me that! My name is Ginna! And what did you have to call them for, anyway? Do we need another lecture on hope and faith?"

Danny flinched noticeably at her words. "I'm sorry," he said to the three standing before him. "She's just not herself lately."

"Maybe I'm finally learning to be myself for a change," said Ginna, stepping closer to them now.

"Perhaps you are, Ginna," came Martina's voice, very calm and even. "I know how difficult that can be, believe me."

Something in her manner seemed to calm Ginna. "I'm sorry," she murmured. "It's so strange to see Jon and Jael here. I'd almost decided it was all just a dream. It seems so long ago now." Her voice tapered into a wistful tone.

"Time is a very relative thing," said Jon. "Who can say what time has done in its many flowing directions since last we talked?"

"I can see that Daniel is taller," Jael said. "He's almost as tall as I am."

"So he is," Jon agreed. "Now, why have you both called us this time?"

"You mean I called, too?" Ginna asked incredulously.

"It appears so, since Martina is here," said Jon.

"Well, I think you can guess why I called," said Danny, glancing at Ginna out of the corner of his eye. "We just don't seem to be communicating the way we used to. Something has come between us."

"Or perhaps something is missing between you," said Martina softly.

"Well, I guess it could be that," Ginna whispered. She was standing next to Danny now, her eyes still fixed on Martina. "Why do I feel I know you already?" she asked at last.

"Our lives may have touched before without our knowing it," Martina replied.

"But how?"

"Is she a forerunner, too?" Danny asked.

"Not exactly," Jon replied. "It's more complicated than that. When we were here before, we told you we were from the future because it was the simplest explanation. But that isn't completely accurate. Let me try another way. Have you heard of parallel universes?"

"No," said Danny.

"I have," Ginna said. "In physics class. Worlds that are sort of next to ours, but we can't see them. One is positive, and the other negative."

"Some are opposites like that, but not all," Jon smiled. He turned to the blinds on the window beside them. "Here's a simple way to explain it. These blinds are colored on one side, white on the other, right? He closed the blinds.

They both nodded.

"This blue side represents your world," he said. "You see only this side. If we were on the other side, we'd see only our world, just the white side."

"I get it!" cried Danny. "When they're opened just the right amount, we can see both sides at once—both worlds."

"That's right, Daniel."

"So when we see you, our worlds are touching," mused Ginna, "The blinds are open."

"Not only when you see us," said Martina. "Sometimes you sense us with other senses than sight."

"And sometimes you can just feel our presence subconsciously without realizing it," Jael added.

"But I sure haven't felt you lately," said Danny. "It's been really lonely around here."

Ginna glared at him. "Well, it's not all my fault."

"Wait," said Jon quietly. "We've come to help as much as we can."

"Are you going to tell us more of your story, Jael?" asked Danny.

"Jon is the story-teller this time," said Jael.

"Yes, now you'll get to see my point of view," Jon nodded. "But I'm not going to just tell you this time. I'm going to take you with me through the blinds to my world. That is, if you're willing to come."

"But how?" Ginna demanded.

"As Jael and Martina," he said softly.

"You mean in their bodies? That's impossible!" she cried.

"I love that word impossible," Jon smiled. "Haven't you read, 'With God, all things are possible'?"

"But I don't want to be lost in someone else's body," she said. "What if we can't come back?"

"It's all right, Ginna," said Danny suddenly, looking into Jael's eyes. "Jael and I have touched many times before, I think. At times, we're almost the same person."

"Remember, we live in parallel worlds," Jon added. "This wouldn't work, otherwise."

"You mean in this world I'm Ginna, but in yours I'm Martina?"

"That's one way to explain it," the tall blond nodded.

"Then right now, am I talking to myself? Looking at myself?"

"Is this any different from looking at yourself in a mirror or talking to yourself when you're alone?"

"Well, I guess it's not. But I'm still afraid," Ginna finally admitted.

Martina stepped forward, taking her hand. "We're all a little afraid of ourselves sometimes, afraid of what we'll find hidden in the deepest recesses of our minds. But it's much better to face those fears and let them flow past us. Then we can learn and move on."

Now Jael stepped forward and took Danny's hand. "Will you do it?" he asked.

"Yes," Danny nodded.

Ginna gave a wordless nod, too.

"Everyone join hands in a circle," Jon said. "And close your eyes."

Even with their eyes closed, they saw a honey-colored light begin to glow in the center of the circle, its warmth radiating toward them, then flowing through them. One moment, Danny was standing between Jael and Martina, with Ginna between Martina and Jon. Then Jael seemed to be gone. Danny found himself holding a larger, stronger hand. It could only be Jon's.

The honey-colored light filled the room now. Someone looking in through the open blinds would have seen three figures standing in a circle, bathed in the rich light. Then the light seemed to flow out of the window, through the blinds, and the figures were gone.

CHAPTER 2

JON'S STORY BEGINS

Maybe the problem was just my restless nature. *[Jon begal]* I wasn't born on Terres, the planet of firm control and discipline, but came there with my parents from the planet of exile, Rubicon. My full name was Jonahkan Son of Jakol, but Mother usually called me Jonah. I often wondered why my name was different from my father's. The custom on Rubicon was for the firstborn son to carry his father's name.

Not many memories of Rubicon are clear to me, just red sand and red stone dwellings, and a pale red sun in the sky which gave poor light—a world of red shadow. I remember red anger in people's voices when they talked, the smoldering of remote colonists in a hostile world, the heat of exiles crying for justice.

And I remember Maia telling Jakol they must find a better life for me, a world with some promise and light. They sold almost everything they owned to buy our passage. We were allowed very little baggage on the great ship, anyway, just what we could carry on our backs. I couldn't carry very much, for I was still quite young.

Yet, I remember the voyage and the great ship as vividly as if it were yesterday. The ship was a behemoth, and the metal shone a silvery-red in our pale sun. The people boarding seemed like tiny insects crawling up the great sloping ramp, far ahead of us in line.

Finally, we were on that ramp ourselves, and the ship loomed high above us, bigger than any building on our planet. It seemed to me something so huge could never leave the ground. I didn't know it then, of course, but it was the small gravity of our planet which made it possible. I did know these great ships were the only way to leave the planet, and they came very rarely to Rubicon. We'd been very fortunate, Maia said, to get a place.

As we walked up the ramp, she was holding tightly to my hand. I could see people who looked as tiny as we did, disembarking down another ramp nearby. She nodded her head to Jakol:

"They look so hopeful now, when they first come."

"Yes." His voice was deep yet speaking softly. "They come as pioneers to a brave new world."

"When they've been here awhile, that will change," she sighed.

"It always does," he nodded.

I looked up at them, puzzled by their soft voices and hard words. And their eyes seemed to say even more to each other than their words expressed.

Then we were inside the great ship. It was dark at first, in a small room where the air seemed to grow heavy. We stepped into a long hallway flooded in bright light. I blinked several times and walked with my eyes squinted closed at first. It was more brightness than I'd ever seen.

All the ship was brightness to me, and for a long time I could barely see because of all the shining metal and bright plastiglas. Even the people seemed to shine. Jakol told me the ones in pale blue uniforms flew the ship. They had special powers, he said.

We had our own small room, but that wasn't until after the ship lumbered into the sky. We lay back in chairs in a huge room for the lift-off, all the people together. I had a harness to hold me in the chair, and I felt very small. There was a shuddering in the walls after awhile, and a pressure on my chest. This lasted for what seemed a long time, and I lay with my eyes closed. Maia held my hand from the chair beside me.

Eventually, the pressure lifted and I felt like I could float. Then something started to spin, but soon that feeling was gone, too. We began walking up what looked like a strange hill, Jakol and Maia holding my hands. It was almost like a dream. The chairs we'd been in were all wrong now, tilted sideways. No one could sit in them now—they would fall out. But all of us were walking up the peculiar smooth hill.

Then we went through a door that hissed open before us, going back into a bright hall, and we were shown our own little room where we could take our baggage off our backs. The light wasn't so bright here, and there were sleeping pads on the floor. I suddenly felt very tired and must have slept for a long time.

I don't know how long we were on the ship—I was too young to count it. I remember many meals eaten, and many times of lying down to sleep. We sometimes sat and played games, and other times one of them would hold me in their lap and tell a story. But there was excitement in the air, for we were flying to a new world somewhere else in the Galaxy.

The very best part was when we could go to the observation dome and watch the Galaxy itself. Each section of the ship had a turn scheduled, so the dome wouldn't get too crowded. I wanted to stand there for as long as I could, gazing silently at the wonders appearing before my eyes—a shining nebula, the dense clusters of stars grouped tightly together, a blazing blue star too bright to look at, or a brooding red giant, so huge and smoldering, with flashes of light and color spilling off its surface.

But the sight which struck me most deeply—and stands out most clearly in my mind even now—was the double star. The clusters and nebulae were more spectacular to some, but I was fascinated with this pair of stars, one white and one orange, rotating around each other. Jakol told me they were attracted to each other by gravity, and wherever one went, the other followed. I didn't understand the forces then, but it was a wonder to me. Even as I grew and learned the science of these things, the fascination of the double star stayed with me.

As I stood watching these wonders, my head full of the tales my parents told of daring and glory, I knew deep inside I belonged in the stars. I dreamed of voyaging across the Galaxy forever, piloting my own great ship, truly at home.

I noticed right away how each time a new star or cluster came into view, there would be a slight blurring at the edges of my vision and a barely perceptible shuddering shift in the ship. It was as though I felt this subconsciously, by instinct. Maia didn't seem to notice it at all. I could tell this by how she talked to Jakol.

"When each new star appears," he said, "We've crossed the GAP."

"How do you know, Jakol? I feel nothing. It seems to be a continual passage to me."

"You can't feel it because you aren't firstborn," he replied. "Only they have the potential for the training."

"That seems odd."

"It's just something someone discovered generations

ago. Without their power, we could never reach most of the stars."

"Why not? We've already seen many stars on this journey. A great ship can cross the Galaxy."

"Yes, it can, but only because of the power to cross the GAP. Each star we see is really a vast distance from the next. It would take our lifetimes and more to make this journey of ours at light-speed. It's impossible to travel as we are now, without the Star Corps and their ability to cross the GAP. Only first-born have the power to learn it."

"How do you know so much, Jakol of Rubicon?" she laughed then.

At this there was a silence, and when I looked up at him, it was as though I could see his eyes speaking words his lips didn't say. There was a hint of red anger there.

"You know what happened to my father, and why he was exiled to Rubicon," he said. "But what you don't know is I was in training for the Star Corps before his disgrace."

His voice broke there, and the red seemed to flood from his eyes to his face. She reached her hand to his cheek and brushed it gently, and when she spoke, her voice was soft and comforting. "I'm sorry," she whispered. "I didn't know. But we're away from that place now. We've bought our own way, and now we have hope for a better life for us all. Perhaps Jonah can even train for the Star Corps."

His eyes brightened. Turning toward me, he smiled, "Yes. Perhaps. He is firstborn, after all."

I smiled back at him, but my eyes were soon back on the stars above and all around us in the dome. 'Yes!' I thought. 'The Star Corps!' My mind filled with high hopes, and I felt as though I were flying across the GAP already. Deep inside, I knew from that moment on I had the power to voyage across the Galaxy to all the stars.

***

Once we got settled on Terres, they enrolled me in Star Corps Academy as soon as I was old enough. I was flying high in my mind then, for I was certain my destiny was to voyage among the stars. Yet, it wasn't long before my high, idealist hopes came crashing down around me like so much ancient glass. I was much too restless and high-spirited for the rigid system of Terres-City, especially the Star Corps. Soon I was branded by the Masters as a rebel and a trouble-maker.

I was always pushing the masters to teach me more and move me beyond my level. I was stymied by their rigid rules and regulations. One event I experienced at the academy stands out as stark and real as if were happening all over again:

I'm standing in the bright hallway of Star Corps Headquarters, before the High Master's door. Somehow, I'd gained an almost unprecedented audience with him. Perhaps my other teachers were overly anxious to get my rebellious actions out of their classrooms and had sent me there—I don't remember for sure.

But I knew this was my chance to do something spectacular with my power, right in front of the High Master himself. I already knew my power to cross the GAP was highly developed for my age, just from watching my classmates. Now if only those in the right places would open their eyes to my skills.

So, I stood waiting before those great double doors. Yet everything about this waiting area seemed to be planned for my discomfort. There was nowhere to sit, and the huge doors gleamed metallically, sending out sparkles of brightness right at eye-level.

Having been born on a dimly-lit planet, my eyes never completely lost their sensitivity to such bright lights. Despite the way those flashes hurt, I found it hard to look away from them, but I forced myself to look at the patterns of color embedded in the floor, instead. I can still see those patterns clearly in my mind—they kept me waiting so long.

'I'm not afraid,' I kept telling myself. 'I just have to make sure to say the right things, so he'll see.'

Then at last came the hiss of the door mechanism, and the snap of a salute. I snapped to attention by reflex, but they'd taken me by surprise. My salute wasn't quick enough to please the guard.

"Look sharp, Cadet!" he snapped. "This is an audience

with none other than the High Master himself. Now, follow me!"

I moved stiffly behind him, feeling more uncomfortable than ever. Silently, in the back of my mind, I felt my resentment welling up. They were using their formality and ceremony as part of a calculated plan to make me as uncomfortable as possible. It was all part of a system designed to elevate themselves by keeping me below them, in what they thought was my place. I became angrier as I thought, 'They're blind to what I can do for them because they refuse to see past their decorum to who I really am.'

Needless to say, with thoughts like this filling my mind, I was not well-prepared to face the High Master.

He was sitting behind a massive desk, with silvery medals shining at his shoulders. The cold glint of metal shone from his eyes, too, along with a blue that matched his uniform. But if his eyes were icy cold, his voice was even colder.

"Tell me, Cadet Jonahkan, what makes you think you're so special? Your teachers are tiring of your selfishness and rebellious ways."

I searched for words to counter him, but my voice seemed to lose itself in the vastness of the room, "Sir, I know what they say about me, but I can do more than any of my classmates. I'm ready for higher levels-"

He began to talk again before I could finish, "You, Cadet, are an upstart. You have no business demanding any special consideration. You've already broken more rules than I can count. The keeping of the rules is a discipline all must learn, including you. The greatest asset of a good Corpsman is to know his place. Do you know yours?"

I wanted to shout, "My place is in the stars! Why can't you see that?" I wanted to fling these words in his stony face, but something in his coldness was chilling me inside, and the words died in my throat. My head was aching now from the brightness assaulting my eyes, and I felt myself grasping inside for some way to show him.

"Well, Jonahkan," he finally demanded, "Do you have anything more to say for yourself?"

His words dropped flatly, as though he didn't really expect any answer. They seemed to fall on the floor at my feet and just lie there. My voice had left me altogether by then, and my heart was pounding. I managed to lift my eyes to glare at him, though. Then I realized the only thing I could do to show him—show them all—that I had the power. I looked hard into those cold blue eyes and then closed my own.

I could hear his surprised voice as I crossed into the GAP. Then I was standing beneath Neptune Spire, and the only sounds around me were distant voices and the rustle of leaves in the wind.

If I'd thought this would impress them, though, I was very wrong. I was branded as an outlaw after this incident and demoted in the Star Corps. Now I was going to have to start over, even further behind than I'd been before.

So, I began to seek any outlet I could find, which meant of course, the Terres Underground. In fact, it was Jason, Raina's brother, who first drew me in. I'll never forget the first time I saw Jason. I'd never met anyone like him before, and it wasn't just the shape of his facial features or his flaming red hair. Outwardly, he seemed to be the epitome of the control the Masters kept trying to teach me. Yet, I could sense a fire within him that matched his hair, and as soon as his shining eyes rested on me, I knew he was a kindred spirit.

My first sight of him came as I made my way home one afternoon, passing a narrow street I'd never really noticed before. Just as I came up to him, he spoke to me, "Greetings, brother." His voice was warm and comfortable sounding. "Would you like to join us for a meeting tonight? I can see you're a seeker. Perhaps we can help."

"How can you know anything about me?" I replied warily. "Who are you?"

"You would know things about me, as well, Jonahkan, if you looked within," he smiled.

I was startled at this—hearing my full name from this stranger's lips. How could he know it? Then a sudden coolness began to flow into my mind, like a searching finger. Instead of fear, though, I felt my own wariness dissolve. And then, as I looked into his gray-blue eyes, I thought he did perhaps have an answer for me. This knowledge came to me in a kind of white flash, an experience not entirely new to me, but soon to be very familiar. I knew who he was, deep in my mind.

"Yes, Jason," I said quietly. "I'll be there."

He didn't seem the least bit startled to hear me say his name. Instead he smiled and touched my shoulder, "I'll see you here at dusk."

The sun set very redly that night, causing all the sky to appear aflame. A red tinge was just beginning to fade from the buildings as I approached the alley. Jason's hair must have caught some of the last light, for it seemed to blaze even brighter than earlier in the day, almost with a light of its own. He smiled that warm smile of his and put his arm around my shoulders.

I didn't feel the least bit uneasy as he led me into the darkness of the narrow street. No light entered between the buildings, until there came a shaft of light from a door opening on our right. Still guided by Jason, I entered a pool of orange light and began to descend a long staircase. At the bottom, a huge, smooth black door stood waiting. With a short word from Jason, it swung open.

The room beyond was a blurred impression of red and black. The ceiling was very high and seemed to disappear above me in mist. The walls were hung with what looked like thick cloth moving slowly, as on a slight breeze. The floor felt very strange—thick and soft like grass, only with a warmer feel, and red in color. Instead of cushions or furniture, the floor itself was pushed into shapes to form sitting or reclining places in a rough semi-circle.

A smoky haze filled the atmosphere, drifting slowly around our heads. My vision began to blur, and by the time Jason seated me, all I could see was a sea of red, flowing with grotesque black shadows.

Voices, speaking so softly and gently. Then the strumming sound of a stringed instrument. The spirit. They were speaking of the spirit, the part of myself so long denied. If I followed my spirit, I'd find my heart's desire, they whispered in my mind. It was as though they came from within myself, rather than outside. This felt so true. I began to sense bonds of tension and rebellion curling, uncurling, and then breaking within me.

One black shadow loomed more sharply now than the rest, and took the shape of a female form, soft in outline, draped in black. Reaching up, I brushed back the upper wrap—it was her hair, long and thick. The warmth of her sent red through me, and I felt something breaking free inside me. I flowed toward her, melting, surging with desires long suppressed. Mist seemed to swirl around my head, and I was rising and falling in some dark sea. Then came the stars. I was voyaging alone, bodily, through the heart of the Galaxy, it seemed. I'd reached my goal among the stars.

***

Red from the rising sun was tingeing the walls as we left the alleyway. Jason shook my hand firmly, smiling a deep warm smile. "We'll see you again," he said. It wasn't a question.

Thus, began my nights in the red blackness and passion of the Terres Underground, the place of release. During the day, I forced myself to assume the role of a disciplined mind. But what a precarious balance this was. I never achieved the control I saw in Jason. By day, my body chafed to be freed of the strict discipline of the mind. And yet, according to the System and under the ever-watchful eyes of the Masters, I couldn't let this conflict show. I didn't always succeed in hiding it.

As evening approached, I longed intensely for the moment when full darkness would settle at last, so I could retreat to the hidden places in the back alleys of the City. There I could do as I wished, following my body's desires wherever they led me.

With most mornings, however, I found myself lying somewhere in gray mist, feeling empty and unsatisfied. My body had its fill, but there seemed to be nothing which could completely satisfy an aching hunger deep within my being, an emptiness that was always there.

As these gray times became more frequent for me, Jason disappeared from my life. No matter where I looked or asked for him, I couldn't find him. People would just smile at me and nod or say something sly about 'Jason's new woman.'

Somewhere during this growing darkness, I met the short, dark young man called Amian. Night after night, he seemed to arrive at the side alley when I did. And soon, he was often there in the grayness of the mornings, watching me with his dark, shining eyes. He never spoke, though, and his silence troubled me.

Finally, one morning he did speak, and though his words made no sense to me then, they rang through my mind into some deeper recesses of my being:

"I will lift up my eyes unto the hills," he said, "From whence cometh my help."

At first, I didn't think he'd meant for me to hear him, his voice barely a whisper. But when I looked toward him, those deep, dark eyes were shining right at me.

"What does that mean?" my voice asked, almost without my willing it.

His eyes flashed and seemed to send a hot, white light right through me. I knew then I was facing someone who wielded great powers.

"It means I see your need," he said in a quiet, even tone. "I can take you to the hills, to the place where your help is, when you're ready."

"Ready for what?"

"To take the step to true freedom. I've watched you here. This place isn't right for you, this double life in City and Underground. I can take you to something far better."

I felt myself nodding involuntarily. It was against all my training to speak of such things. No one spoke of the

Underground in the light of day. Yet I found myself listening intently to Amian.

"I can take you to The People, the Redlarks, as they call us here. That's where you can be free of this double life, this separation of mind and body. With us, your spirit can be truly free."

This was the first time I'd heard of the Redlarks, except for guarded whispers behind hiding palms, "the nonexistent ones in the Wilds—those who have dared to leave."

Amian was still talking, using his power over me well, his voice continuing to calmly tell me about The People. I listened to his every word, enraptured. This did indeed sound like a much better way to live—in freedom to obey the spirits, with The People in the Wilds. And his timing was helped by some force of fate. I often wondered if he knew, for this was just after my mother died. So, I listened to him with all my heart that morning, and knew I was already making my choice.

["What happened to your mother?" Ginna asked.

There was a long silence, and when she looked at Jon, she saw tears in his eyes.

"Oh, I'm sorry! I didn't mean to make you cry."

Jon brushed them angrily away. "Sometime I may be able to tell it, but not yet," he muttered.

Then he resumed his story.]

When Amian stopped speaking, his eyes rested on me silently for a long time. And I could feel a strange stirring within me. How could I refuse a chance at a better life away from this burdensome city? Yet, I didn't speak, for some little idea kept trying to push itself into my mind, trying to force Amian's influence out. Perhaps he saw this for he suddenly took both my hands in his.

"Close your eyes," he said, "And open your mind. I know you can cross the GAP with me."

I'd still been teaching myself to use this power of the firstborn, the power to make jumps across expanses of space and time, but my attempts weren't at full Star Corps level yet. As soon as I crossed with Amian, I knew he was a master of the power.

Instantly, we were standing atop Neptune Spire on a bright cloudless afternoon. He smiled up at me, his dark eyes dancing.

"Can all Redlarks do that?" I asked breathlessly.

"Only firstborn, of course, like you," he smiled. "We can help you develop your powers, this one and many others."

This was a promise I couldn't resist, a way to develop my powers without the long, grinding discipline of the Star Corps.

"You could take me there, just like that, in the twinkling of an eye?" I asked in awe.

"Then you'll come now?" he asked.

"What's the price? There's always a price for anything worth having."

He nodded at this. "Total change will come. To Terres-City you'll be gone forever, declared non-existent, and never permitted see anyone you knew here again. It's forbidden. And besides, you'll forget all your past."

It didn't sound like a high price to me then. At that point, there was no one left I cared for in the City—my mother was gone. And after what Amian told me, the thought of being non-existent to this place sounded wonderful.

"You must become a new person, with a new name. What do you say?"

"Yes, of course!"

His eyes were still on the distant peaks. "I have some words from an ancient book, which I believe are your song: 'I will lift up my eyes unto the hills, from whence cometh my help'."

"I heard you say those words before. What book are they from?"

"Just one of the ancient writings. Do you read?"

"Yes, I know some," I replied. But my mind wasn't thinking of books then—it was listening to those words echo back and forth in my thoughts. "Yes, those words are for me," I said at last.

"So that is your song. And now your name—Jonah."

I started inwardly, 'How does he know the special name only my mother called me? He even pronounced it correctly: Jah-nah, not Joe-nah.'

"That is your name, isn't it?" he smiled. "Someday you'll learn its full meaning."

There was a long silence between us. So much was happening so quickly, but my mind seemed quiet, and I felt deep inside that I'd come face-to-face with my destiny at last.

"I'm ready to go, right now," I said.

He smiled and closed his eyes. A hand touched my head, and then it became a breeze ruffling my hair. We were standing in a green forest clearing at the base of the Peaks. So, I came to The People.

CHAPTER 3

DON'T PUSH THE RIVER

The People took pride in living off the land. Their huts were of materials from the forest, and so were their clothes. The Wilds of Terres provided amply for most of their needs. Having lived in the City for so long, I'd forgotten how it was to live close to the land.

Being back there in the Wilds brought some of my most distant memories back to mind, memories of my childhood on a lonely red planet at the edge of the Galaxy, and of a life that was more basic, if hard—and freer. Because of this, I began to feel at home with The People.

Amian stayed long enough to help me begin my own hut, showing me how to use a large axe to fell trees and hew timbers. He made it clear to me it was part of his responsibility as the one who brought me. Once a frame was up, we wove strips of bark into hangings for the walls. A softer type of bark was used to make my new clothes.

With my new name and my new clothes, I felt I fit in this place, like I could melt into the forest unseen.

The day he left, he brought Daiah, whose name meant Compassion, he said. She was just his height with dark hair falling in soft curls around her shoulders. I wondered if they were related. But who could tell, since everyone forgot their past here? Her long-lashed eyes were so blue I could see them from a distance as she approached. My blood warmed with a spreading fire. He put her hand in mine and said, "This is Daiah. She'll be your teacher now."

"I'll finish the thatching for your roof," she said in a deep-toned voice, "So you can bid farewell to Amian."

I stood awestruck, as she took the sack of thatch I'd been gathering. She spread its contents before the hut's door, and her fingers moved deftly and silently, weaving.

Amian guided me by the arm to the edge of the clearing around the hut. "A good choice I made for you, eh?" he smiled.

"Is she mine then?"

"She'll stay with you as long as her spirit wills it. People don't always belong to others here."

I nodded, realizing I still had much to learn.

"Are you returning to Terres-City?" I asked.

"Yes, as an unknown again. No one will know I've been sent, until I choose to tell the ones who are chosen, like you."

"If you should see Jason…"

"Stop!" he said suddenly, his voice sharp and his eyes full of surprise. When he spoke again, his voice had an ominous ring, "You should have forgotten him by now. You must forget."

"I'm sorry," I murmured.

"He's from your past, which must be left behind forever. Besides, he's not one of us. He had his chance."

"Is there any hope for him then?"

"Why should that worry you?" The steely cold in his voice made me feel very uneasy.

"Amian, I'm sorry if I said something wrong. I still have a lot to learn here." I tried to smile.

A slow smile cracked his face then. "Well, you just let Daiah take care of you. She's the best teacher I know."

"Will I see you again?"

"Only if the spirits will it."

He was smiling at me as his eyes closed. Then he was gone.

***

I learned much from Daiah—like how to find food, clothing, and other necessities there in the Wild. As I look back, I see her as the only person among The People who kept some spirit of peace and innocence in that place of dark, seething forces. I tried to keep myself content to stay with her at the edge of the Camp, seeing few others and speaking to almost no one else. But it seemed as time went on, this life became too quiet for me.

Her quiet spirit left a lasting respect in me, but it couldn't protect me from the hideous dark powers I fell prey to.

Because fall prey I did. Even with Daiah, I could sense dark forces creeping under the surface. She could seem so unspoiled and innocent when I took her in my arms, but I knew it was just part of her spell. She must have been with others before me. She knew so much that I didn't, and Amian seemed to have known her very well.

I guess it was her quietness that kept the veil of innocence intact for her, and the way she hovered in her own little world, away from the forces and activities which centered in the Pavilion of the Priests.

I didn't want to go to that tent—it seemed there was some dark foreboding in my heart about the place. Yet despite this, or perhaps because of it, I became increasingly restless and began to wander far and wide in search of something, I knew not what. I roamed the forests, explored the rivers, and climbed the mountains. But that Pavilion kept drawing me back.

One day, I prepared a pack-sack with food for a longer trek and set out as soon as Daiah left the hut to gather fruits for us. I watched her go in silence, not sure why I hesitated to tell her where I was going.

The sun was wonderfully warm that day, and I worked my way through the foothills toward the tallest of the crags in the long range which brooded over us. I decided I had to see what was on the other side of these Peaks at the edge of the world. The climb was slow and steady for most of the day. My breath began to labor as I reached higher altitudes, but I pressed on. The food in my sack sustained me for the first day. But darkness overtook me before I scaled the last heights. I decided I must rest and try to reach the summit the next day.

While I lay on the open ground, the sky grew darker, and I saw stars winking in the blackness. First the brightest ones appeared, and then many others joined them. I'd never seen so many stars. The sky in the City had never been ablaze like this—there was too much light there. Now I felt I was gliding through these stars in some kind of boat, drifting and just staring up in awe.

The words of a song I'd heard Daiah sing echoed in my mind: 'The heavens are telling the glory of God.'

I must have fallen asleep then because the next thing I knew the sky was lightening, and pink clouds were drifting across my view. Finishing off what food was left, I set out again, working my way to the final cliff face that stood between me and the top of the mountain.

For the last thousand meters of the climb, I couldn't see anything besides my feet as they sought the next safe place to step. Then suddenly, all around me was sky. I was finally standing on top of the ridge at its highest point. Behind me was the green valley with the camps of The People.

Before me was a flat barren plain. There seemed to be no inhabitants and little vegetation, a very forbidding place. Yet a voice deep inside was telling me I would someday be down there. Right now though, I needed to head back to the Camp. I'd seen the future, but it wasn't time for it yet.

And so, I descended, feeling drawn by a force stronger than I'd ever felt before. Despite what my conscious mind kept saying, my feet kept walking toward the Temple Pavilion. At last, I could see the door of the huge tent, and noticed with a shock it was made of a thick black material that could only have come from the City. So much for living off the land. This made me angry, and I turned on my heel and started back toward my hut.

I'd almost reached the familiar little clearing when Daiah stepped right in front of me. She was almost blocking my way, and I didn't understand it.

"What's going on?" I asked.

"Did you see what you expected from your mountain-peak?"

I wasn't sure if she was trying to change the subject or misunderstood my question. I just shrugged an answer, "I could see the other side—far and wide."

"The way your heart seeks," she murmured.

"What?"

"I know your heart," she continued. "It's great and wide like the world, not content with the small, like mine. You search and crave, for you're made for the greater things, rather than the small."

"How do you know?"

"I've been told."

Something in the tone of her answer made me wonder whether the voices telling her this were human or spirits. "What are you saying, Daiah?"

"You must go. Don't deny the call within you. You're meant for higher things. And when you're up there in your place, I'll be down here in mine."

"Please, come with me," I cried suddenly, and grabbed her hand.

She pulled back from me. "No, Jonah. I'm not meant to be with you any longer. There's another for you now."

Her hand brushed quickly at her cheek, and I saw tears shining there. I reached out to touch those flushed cheeks, to gather her to me and kiss the tears away. But as soon as I moved toward her, she turned and ran. In less than an instant, she'd disappeared into the trees.

I stood there in silence, my heart pounding in confusion. Had someone told her she must leave me? Were we both being manipulated by some outside power? And was this power the so-called spirits, or some person who wished to control me? At these thoughts, I felt panic well up inside, but there seemed to be no place to run. Then that strange feeling returned, the pull drawing me ever closer to the Temple.

My feet took me back to the center of the Camp, where I stood staring at the black door. It was getting toward evening, I realized, as I saw shadows lengthening across the cloth walls before me. Again, I tried to turn and walk away, and this time my way was blocked by a tall, lithe woman.

From the instant I saw her, I was captivated—first by the flaming amber of her hair as it caught the last rays of the sun, and then by those piercing green eyes, which seemed to gleam like a feier-cat's in the dark. She didn't say a word or touch me, but I could feel cool fingers reaching into my mind, turning my head to follow her every move as she walked toward the door. 'Do I have any right to claim her?' I wondered

When she was almost to the door, she stopped and looked back as if to ask why I was still standing there. Feeling embarrassed by her stare, I turned to leave. But as I did so, I saw the letters in the dust, formed by a pattern carved in her sandal, "Follow me."

Again, came that feeling of cool fingers in my mind, and I turned to obey those words. As I did so, there came a soft throaty laugh, barely audible. Yet within my head it seemed to echo in eerie overtones. Soon I was beside her at the door.

"It's time you joined the Rituals, Jonah," she whispered, in a voice which sent thrills coursing through my body. "I'm Zhabet, your guide." Again, came that eerie echoing in my mind.

When I entered the dark, smoke-filled pavilion, I entered another world—the world of unbridled spirits, long-suppressed in my life, but freed here in all their awesome and fearful power.

I'm not even sure how much time passed for me in there—perhaps days or weeks, or only one night. But the memory is just a blur for me now, grays and reds, enshrouded in black. I remember watching priests performing rituals over bodies laid out on the altar. I can see in my mind the seething forms, as spirits were called forth. And then there came the calling of the most powerful one they called the Great Spirit of The People—a terrible vision of black, rimmed with flames. Sometimes Zhabet was at my side; sometimes I was alone in a sea of darkness.

Then I'm in a small boat on a great river. Fierce rapids are splashing water into my eyes and voices are cheering from the shore. Blinking, I suddenly see other boats around me, and I realize I'm in a race I must win. Yet the harder I try to push ahead with my paddle, the thicker the water seems, like I'm fighting a great wall of force.

Then Zhabet's voice calls from the shore, "Don't push the river, Johan. Go with the flow."

I wonder why she's calling me that name but have no time to figure it out. What does she mean by "the flow"? Anything I want to say is pushed back by a sudden splash of icy water in my face.

Then a bright, golden light pierces the gloom around me, flowing ahead of me, shimmering on the waves of water. I stop pushing the paddle so deep and use it instead as a rudder to steer myself into that golden stream. I begin to move ahead of the rest of the boats, sliding quickly and easily through the foaming rapids.

The wind rushes through my hair and whirrs in my ears, like I'm flying. And when I look down, I see not water but darkening light flecked with hundreds of sparkling stars. I'm floating into that night sky I saw on my trek. Great cheers engulf me, and I know I've won the race. As the wind swirls faster and faster around me, it begins to darken, pulling me deeper inside.

When I woke again, I felt Zhabet's cool hands on my chest.

"Why did you call me Johan?"

"It means 'The one who shows the way,' and I know you'll do that someday," she whispered in my ear.

"How can I show the way when I don't even know it myself?" I replied. "My name is Jonah, not Johan."

"But Jonah means 'One who runs from God'," she giggled.

"Well that sounds more like me," I sighed. "All my life I seem to be running from something."

"We shall see," she breathed.

Power was flowing all around me, drifting past my head like the smoke of a fire. Or was it the haze of those black and red nights of the City Underground? I looked up and saw firelight dancing in her hair, setting it into shimmering flame. Her eyes were shrouded by her lashes, but when they opened suddenly, fire seemed to flow into me.

"You are mine," she whispered in my ear.

My hands were beneath her robe, caressing skin that was smooth and warm. She came to me with the gentlest of motions, and I found her lips with mine. It was as though I'd never had a woman before. This was as different from the Underground as day is different from night.

***

After this, she took me to her hut and began to teach me the ways of mixing herbs for potions, and of weaving spells. She seemed the answer at last to that hunger deep inside me.

Gradually, I realized she saw in me an answer to her hunger, as well. She was hungry for power, the more the better, in any form. And apparently, she thought I had the potential to take her higher.

I often wondered what it was these women saw in me. What made them think I had all this power? But unlike the gentle Daiah, who spoke in vague mystic phrases, Zhabet had more concrete ideas and goals in her sights. She finally revealed to me that she was grooming me to challenge the High Chieftain himself.

So, she taught me the power of influencing minds, the ways of commanding with my voice, and the art of combat with the scim-blade, a fearsome hooked thing with several sharp prongs. She knew I'd need all these skills in the Duel. The High Chieftain at that time was Dirkhan, a tall, powerfully built man, very handsome, and a strong leader. I didn't like the idea of killing him—for the Duel was always to the death—but I liked the idea of dying even less.

Such was the power of a woman to drive a man for her ambitions, and especially the power the bewitching Zhabet had over me.

When the time came to challenge Dirkhan, she prepared me with a strong spell, so I went into that Duel like a madman, raving and enraged, but still focused on the goal. He didn't have a chance, for it wasn't against me alone he battled, but against the spirits Zhabet called to empower me.

Thus, I became High Chieftain with this witch as my Consort. She'd taught me to find the golden flow of fate in my dream river and launched us both into it.

While actually pushing me with her powers, she somehow convinced me we weren't pushing the river—that we were flowing as things were meant to. But soon, fate proved her wrong.

CHAPTER 4

THE SIGN AND THE RETURN

The time of my chieftainship with Zhabet is the darkest part of any of my memories. I think it's the mercy of time to blot out memories too dark and horrible to bear. Yet, there are some images branded on my mind, hot and searing, perhaps as a warning of how dark the heart can be when controlled by the unleashed spirits from below.

I'm not even sure how long my reign of terror lasted—long enough that The People came to fear me. I like to think it was really Zhabet's doing, for she was the source of my deepest power. I was a tool in her hands, yet I know I bear the guilt, as well.

The usual challengers of a new High Chieftain soon emerged, and I defeated each of them in their turn, with the scim-knife and the power of words over minds. A quiet fear enveloped all the Camp, each one returning to their own place again, with no one daring to cross me.

Then she became pregnant with my child. With this, I learned something very strange about the culture of The

People. Children were rarely born there, so I knew some forms of contraception must be in use. But when a woman did conceive, all medical ideas and safeguards were immediately thrown to the wind. Now everything was in the hands of the spirits, they said. I could only shake my head; there was no arguing with Zhabet and her maidens.

Soon she began to get a hollow, glassy look in those green eyes. I tried to shrug it off, thinking perhaps all women changed like this when they were with child. Still, the circles under her eyes darkened with each passing day. If I ever asked her about it, she would just laugh lightly:

"You've no need to fear, Jonah. The spirits and the stars agree. I will bear you a son who will be High Chieftain after you. No one will ever again challenge our power, or our children's."

But she was wrong. Perhaps the spirits turned against her in her insatiable lust for power. I don't know how or why everything went wrong, but it did. She began to be pale as a ghost, and I discovered she was bleeding. Soon she was in bed all the time, unable to move. I could hardly sit beside her, watching the way the pain tortured her. Yet still she refused any medical aid, crying instead to the spirits to deliver her.

I found myself lashing out at them angrily, too, for there was nothing else I could do. And still she lay in agony, trying to hold back the screams. It was a relief when she finally died.

As I sat there alone with her now-silent body, it was a bleak and gray day outside. I could hear the wind moaning around the chieftain's hut and rain lashing across the roof. The chill seemed to reach through the walls and into my heart. I was more alone than I'd ever been in my life. Zhabet with her powers had totally possessed me, and now that she—and my child—were gone, I was nothing but an empty shell.

Then I realized suddenly the main promise which brought me here—learning to cross the GAP—had been unfulfilled. No one here seemed to know any more about it than I did. 'Amian lied!' I thought bitterly. 'He used my heart's desire against me. Do I even *have* the power to cross the GAP anymore? If not, I'm helpless here.'

Beside her dead body, I knew this emptiness was the result of my surrender to those dark forces. My mind could go back in thought, but it had no power left to move bodily from this room of death and dread. It seemed I'd truly lost all my own power.

I knew if anyone found out how powerless I was, I'd soon be dead, too. So, it was in a desperate attempt at self-preservation that I dreamed up the idea of my search for the Sign. Using what little power of words I could muster, I made a proclamation:

"The stars have lied—we've somehow angered the spirits—and now it's my duty as the bereaved to find the way to appease them. I'll return to the City, seeking the

Sign I know is to come, a Sign revealing the true will of the spirits once again."

In the dead silence following my speech, it was the gentle Daiah who first stood by me, "Jonah speaks the truth!" she cried. "We must find the new way, through his Sign."

Thankfully, others followed her example and supported my plan.

And so, I prepared to make a journey few of The People ever made—back into the City. I appointed Rigan, the captain of my guard, to act as High Chieftain in my stead, hoping he didn't have the same power-lust as Zhabet.

When all was ready, I set out on foot across the Wilds—spending many days to cross the distance Amian had brought me across in an instant. No one asked why I chose not to cross the GAP, which was lucky, because I didn't want to admit I was unsure of my power.

Once in Terres-City, I had no idea what to do or where to go, for I was a stranger there. I knew no one, and no one knew me. So, I found myself a small room above some shops at a corner of two narrow streets. And then I just waited—not knowing what, if anything, would happen next.

My idea of the Sign was just a ploy to get me out of The People's sight, or so I thought. But perhaps some spirit had spoken to me one last time when the idea came, for I began to have strange feelings something spectacular really was about to happen. My expectancy began to focus on the time of sunset.

As I waited, there were old familiar patterns all around—the secret rendezvous of so many with the Underground. I had no desire to join them, my heart and mind now hollow and empty. The physical release of those dark places had become mere child's play to me, compared to the orgies and rituals of The People.

In fact, I didn't know what I wanted anymore. I could never be part of the City again—I was just an unknown shadow, lurking in a dim corner. And I could see the false-hood of the System much too clearly. I knew The People were correct in not denying the spirit or separating mind and body. But there was something wrong with them, too. Powers were being unleashed there which should be controlled somehow. I knew I'd been swept away by evil in the Camp. But my answer wasn't here in the City, either.

'Is there any answer at all?' I often wondered to myself.

At night, the stars peered down from the sky and mocked me, so dim in the City lights. Here I was, bound to this planet, when deep inside I longed to be out there, voyaging among the stars.

***

Now here I was—unable to return to the Star Corps, a stranger in my own City, and fled from the dark forces

I feared in The People. There seemed to be no place for me, or my dream, in all the Universe. I was at the lowest point of my life then and began to wonder if there was any reason for me to go on living. But I didn't even have the strength or courage to end it all myself. I was paralyzed in despair.

Then one night, an old desire finally took hold of me. As I looked down at the narrow street below my small lodging, I saw a familiar shock of flaming red hair and became immediately alert and excited. Without even thinking what I was doing, I raced down to the street. Suddenly, the only thing I cared about was seeing someone I recognized, after such a long time of utter loneliness.

"Jason!" I cried, speaking for the first time in ages.

He turned in great surprise, "Jonahkan!"

For some reason, I cringed at hearing my City name, and put my hand up to stop him. His eyes looked at me full of questions.

Suddenly I wasn't even sure what to call myself. The name Jonah didn't seem right in the City, either. Finally, I murmured, "Just call me Jon from now on."

And so, I became Jon for the rest of my life.

"Is there somewhere we can go to talk?" I asked him.

"Anywhere!" he grinned. "What's your pleasure?"

"No really, Jason. I just want to talk right now. But I'm not sure I should even be talking to you."

"What do you mean?"

"I've been to the Redlarks, and I'm told it's forbidden to come back."

"Oh, don't listen to those fools," he laughed. "I'm not afraid of them."

"Well, I really do need to talk to someone," I sighed, though all the while Amian's warning rang in my ears.

By the look on Jason's face, I knew it would be difficult to explain any of this to him. But then I thought, 'If it doesn't bother him to have contact, why should I worry? I've been so lonely, anyone will help at this point.'

So, I took him up the narrow stairs to my room above the street.

This was the beginning of a new and strange sort of relationship. We'd sit and talk for hours, for there was little else we could agree to. I had no interest in his Underground anymore, and I couldn't explain to him what I'd experienced. Still the talk helped to fill my emptiness. He talked of news in the City, and I tried to explain some of the ways of The People. He didn't seem to understand much, though.

"Those are like Old Ways," he sneered, when I talked of living off the land. "We've advanced so far past all that."

"Sure!" I'd retort. "You're so advanced you have to find a way to release all the forces you've pent up and denied. You lie to yourselves by day, saying you've disciplined the mind. Then you turn around and lie to yourselves at night when you think you're hiding in the Underground. There's no real fulfillment there. You're trapped in a two-faced lie."

He'd always give some answer about how the nights made the days possible. "And besides," he added, "Aren't the power and might of Terres-City a testimony to the rightness of the System?"

"Power and might aren't necessarily a testimony to the rightness of anything," I replied.

"Oh, I suppose the Redlarks have found some other testimonies then," he said.

Here I'd always find myself hedging. He was right. I'd seen no other justifications with The People—only the might of power. And yet, I wished deep inside there was some other way of doing things, somewhere in the Universe.

Once I tried to change the subject by asking him about his new woman I heard about. "What is she like?" I asked. "I saw nothing of you before I left the City. She must be very special to keep *you* out of the Underground."

His eyes looked very sad for a moment, and then he spoke with anger. "Martina left me," he said. "For the Redlarks. I don't suppose you saw her?"

"No, I'm sorry. I didn't meet any new girls before I came back. And she wouldn't keep her City name, anyway. What did she look like?"

"She was gorgeous," he smiled sadly. "Long dark hair,

beautiful green eyes, perfect figure. And what a lover!"

The depth of emotion in his voice cut into me. "I'm so sorry, Jason. Why did she leave?"

"I don't know. Her oldest brother died in the wars. Her second brother left for the Inland Raiders. All she had left was a little brother who wasn't in school yet. Their mother was put in the Institute."

"Like mine." Those words slipped from me before I could stop them.

Jason seemed not to notice, though, as he went on, "Her family had some strange ways. Then someone turned in a report on their books, and their place was trashed. By then, only Jael, the youngest, was left at home, so I convinced him to come stay with us. I won't be surprised if he tries to go find his sister."

"That would be very risky. How old is this little brother?" I said.

"Oh, about ten or eleven Standard Years. He's finally started school."

"I sure hope he doesn't try to go alone," I said. I had no idea at that time how closely I'd become connected with these people in the future.

Jason and I never got very far with each other in our discussions, whether at my lodgings or his home. He never seemed to understand what I felt were such logical arguments. And I suppose he thought the same of me. Still, these times were good for me, and in a way, we became friends again, though philosophically we were at a stalemate.

Not long after this, I first met Jael at Jason's house. You've heard this part of the story told very well by Jael, so I won't repeat it.

[A great shudder suddenly shook Jon's body, and a honey-colored light flared in the air.

"Jon, are you all right?" cried Martina.

"Huh? Oh, yes." Jon took a ragged breath. "I'm just so tired all of a sudden—have to rest."

"I guess these memories have become too much for him to bear, and he had to let them out," said Jael. "I've never heard most of them before."

Jon kept his eyes closed for a long time. Then at last he spoke again, "I couldn't keep these things inside any longer. They would have eaten me alive." He smiled a wan smile. "I think I can go on now. In fact, it's time for all of us to begin our journey together from here."]

CHAPTER 5

THE FAR EDGE OF NOWHERE

We were camped on the edge of the Far Wilds, my companions and I—right at the base of the towering peaks looming at the edge of the world. But that world was behind us now and out of sight.

The Far Wilds! The thought of them filled me with fear and anticipation. No one knew what lay out there, for no one lived there. As far as I knew, no one on Terres had even been there. But it held a fascination for me, ever since I'd stood on the highest peak one day years ago, looking out at this vast empty-looking plain, and thinking:

'This is the part of Terres I don't know yet. All the rest—the City and The People—I've seen. And there's nothing for me here, so I must go forward into this unknown.'

Yet I hadn't gone forward into the Far Wilds then. I went back down to the Redlarks—who called themselves The People—drawn by my fate, perhaps, and by the power the witch had held over me.

Now the memory of Zhabet made me shiver, and it wasn't just from the early morning chill. The first light began to creep over the peaks behind us. Jael and Martina stirred and yawned as I stoked the small cooking fire. To force those dreadful images of Zhabet out of my mind, I watched these two who so recently became such an important part of my life.

Martina was slender, with sleek dark hair that hung long. She'd allowed me to take her as my Consort when I was High Chieftain of The People. I knew she'd belonged to Rigan before that, and probably others, as well. Yet, I was finding that I cared for her in a different way than any other woman in the Camp of The People. With others, in the past, there'd only been floods of passion, but it wasn't like that now. Maybe I was just beginning to understand love.

Jael was her younger brother, and I sometimes fondly called him Little Brother, not because we were blood relations but because of all we'd been through together. Jael seemed young, due to his small size, but he had intelligence and wisdom far beyond his years. Perhaps this was partly due to Feier, his telepathic feier-cat, a creature of the Wilds tamed as a pet. In fact, it was Feier who first brought us together, back in the City. That was the first time I tried to flee the Redlarks, though.

I shrugged to brush these thoughts away, and we began the first day of our trek into the unknown.

When night fell, seemingly too soon, we had to stop and make camp. I didn't know the terrain here at all, and we couldn't travel in the dark. I had very mixed feelings as I watch my two companions.

'I'm taking a huge risk,' I thought, 'Involving the people dearest to me in this strange experiment of merging Ginna's consciousness with Martina's—and Danny's with Jael. Yet, all four are willing.' I crawled into my bark blanket and tried to get some sleep.

Sleep wouldn't come, though. My mind kept dwelling on the predicament we were in now. We couldn't go back, but was there anything ahead except empty wilderness? It struck me that here I was running again. My name of Jonah—one who runs from God—seemed to fit me all too well. Perhaps that's another reason I changed it to just 'Jon.'

Another dark thought was whether I'd be able to regain my power to cross the GAP, now that I was away from The People. It had almost come back to me in the City, and this morning I felt the power deep within myself, waiting for the right time. Perhaps this was one thing I'd finally learned—not to push ahead too soon—not to push the river.

Somehow, I must have finally slept, for the next thing I saw was the sun rising again in the west. 'Perhaps the days are still shortened by the effect of our planet's new Double-star,' I thought. Then I saw Jael sit up sleepily.

As I looked into his green eyes, I realized he had a very special power in his love. He'd brought his sister back from her oblivion to the dark spirits of the Redlarks, and somehow reached me, too.

"So what do we do now?" he asked.

"All we can do is to continue east into the Far Wilds."

"But what's out there, Jon?" He pointed toward the broad, flat plain reaching before us.

"I don't know," I answered honestly. "And the only way to find out is to keep going." I stood and stretched as I spoke.

"Yeah, we can't just sit here on the edge of nowhere," he agreed.

Martina stood now also, but I could see by her eyes that she wished there were some other choices open to us. I wanted to reach out and give her a hug, to try to reassure her. But I wasn't sure what her reaction would be so soon after her delivery from the spirits' possession, so I restrained myself.

"Let's have a bit of food before we do anything else," I suggested.

"Now *that's* a sensible suggestion," she said and quickly began to pull some food out of the pack-sacks I'd filled for us before leaving the Camp.

After a brief meal, we resumed working our way

across the great flat expanses of the Far Wilds. There were few rises of any kind to get our bearings, just an unending expanse of plains. Trees grew sparsely, so as our journey progressed, we spent many a chilly night, when we could find nothing to burn for fuel. Soon our meager store of food began to dwindle, but for a time, I refused to think of this, hoping we would find something edible eventually.

At night, I'd lie awake while the others slept, just staring up at the stars. They seemed so bright here in the wild places, but they were still far away, unreachable. I'd spent most of my life trying to reach those stars, but now it seemed I never would. Instead, I just kept leaving places—first Rubicon, then the Star Corps, and the City, and now The People—twice. I'd always told myself subconsciously these places were not where I was meant to be, that they were nowhere. I kept hoping that my 'Somewhere' was still out there ahead of me, out there in the stars.

On some nights, though, my hopes would fade, and I'd wonder if I was just wandering aimlessly through life. Was there really any meaning after all?

At last one night, I seemed to reach the very bottom of a pit of despair. Perhaps it was partly the clouds that had moved in, obscuring the stars. Cold wind was blowing, as well, and all of us were huddled close to try to keep warm. Suddenly I felt the warm touch of a rough tongue licking my hand. I drew up in surprise to see Feier sitting there.

Usually, he stayed close to Jael all the time. I let him climb under my blanket, and the presence of his soft warmth began to bring some comfort.

'You mustn't despair, Jon,' his words came softly in my mind. 'Jael and Martina are depending on you. They trust you to lead them to a better place.'

'But how can I?' I cried back to him in thoughts. 'I don't even know where I'm going.'

'Still you mustn't give up, just because you can't see what lies ahead.'

'Can you?' I had a sudden hope that perhaps he could see something of our future.

'Not any better than you can,' he replied.

My heart sank.

'Yet,' he continued, 'I know there's hope ahead. Only those who know what lies ahead without a doubt have the right to despair. Imagine knowing every step before you even took it. *That* would be a reason to despair. There would be no opportunity for choices, for making decisions. All you could do is trudge on the path, always knowing what would happen next. There would be no surprises, no wonder, and no hope.'

'I've never thought of it that way,' I said to myself. 'I guess I thought it would be easier to know what was ahead, to not have to risk making wrong decisions.'

'Some would say that, but they'd be missing the great mystery of time,' Feier went on. 'If we don't know the future, then we cannot know if it will be good or bad until it comes. And since both are possible, we can have *hope* for the good.'

I was full of wonder at the little feier-cat's grasp of these things. 'How do you know this?'

'I'm not sure, Jon. I just know there's a reason I'm here with you now, to remind you that you *do* have the power to reach your dream of the stars. Each of us will do what we can and try not to let the others down. We each have strengths that together will make us all stronger.'

At this, I lay in my blanket in silence for a long time. As I turned his words over in my mind, I found I wanted to believe them and to follow them. And I realized this was the only alternative to total despair. If I'd been alone that night, I might have abandoned myself to despair, wandering alone in those Far Wilds until I died. But now I saw clearly how these others were entrusted to my care for a reason. I really had no alternative than to assume my responsibility, but now I knew I'd also have their help.

'My mother used to call me Jonah,' I said to Feier at last. 'Zhabet told me it means "One who runs from God". What do you think—am I just a Jonah?'

'Did you know the man called Jonah in The Book turned back to God after he ran, and went where God sent him, after all? He became "The One Who Tells the Truth of God".'

'Really?'

'Yes.'

'Well, I guess I'll have to keep searching for that Truth, too.'

'That sounds like a good start, Jon,' he purred, as we settled down into sleep.

***

And so, we continued across those bleak and faceless plains. There seemed to be so few landmarks to aim for, that I used the stars as our main source of navigation. This involved a lot of guesswork, since the constellations and patterns had changed with the arrival of our sun's new partner. Still, I felt confident we weren't going in circles.

One day, a small rise appeared ahead of us, and we made for it with excitement. As we gradually neared it, and distinct features began to emerge from the sameness of brown and tan, we could see that there were even a few scraggly trees clustered at this base.

"We'll have a nice warm fire tonight," I cried, to encourage all of us. "Let's make it to that grove by nightfall."

By pushing ourselves, we did make it just after sunset.

Never had a fire seemed so warm and cheerful, after all those cold, bleak nights. We sat up late into the evening, watching the orange flames dance, smelling the acrid smoke, and then watching as the red embers faded one by one. Jael was the first to curl up and doze off, with

Feier nestled next to him.

But I wasn't sleepy yet. I felt warmer than I had in a long time, and my heart was even warmer than the glowing red coals before my eyes. Gradually, I moved closer to Martina, feeling her presence call back feelings for her I'd known ever since first seeing her in the Camp.

When I was sure Jael was asleep, I reached for her hand. Immediately I could feel her muscles tense.

"What's the matter?" I asked softly. "I've never hurt you, even when I was High Chieftain. You know I never would."

"I'm not your Consort anymore," she hissed. "Just leave me alone."

"You don't have to have sex with me," I whispered. "I just care for you. Perhaps I even love you."

"What do you know of love?" she snapped.

I fell silent, and then drew myself away from her slightly, which was very hard to do. "I want to learn what love really is," I said at last. "Jael has helped me see it's more than just a body-lust, that it goes all the way into a person's soul."

"I've heard you call Jael 'Little Brother'," she whispered. "So I know you've learned some things about other kinds of love. Why can't you think of me that way, and love me as a sister?"

An ember in the fire flared just then, sending up a blue flame and casting a dim light on her face. There were tears glistening at the corners of her eyes, and I wanted desperately to kiss them away.

"It's just so hard to love you as a sister when you've been much more to me before."

"That was another place and time," she said in a faraway voice. "It doesn't seem right now." Then suddenly her voice changed, and she sounded frustrated, "Oh, I can't explain how I feel!"

There was an undertone of anguish in her voice that cut me deeply. I wasn't sure if I was the cause of it, but I wished desperately to help cure it. Yet I knew if I reached for her now, she'd only pull away again.

"Martina," I said hoarsely, "I want to learn to *really* love you, that's all."

"If you do love me, you'll wait until I can sort things out—until I understand all these messed-up feelings I have." She was looking me in the eye for the first time. "Please…"

Again, I felt an almost overwhelming desire to take her in my arms and comfort her. But the look of fear and confusion in her eyes stopped me. I knew somehow I couldn't smooth away this pain. It was a task too great for me. I sat with her in silence until the last ember died. Then we crept off to our own blankets.

But I couldn't go to sleep. As I looked up at the stars, the light of fear and pain that I'd seen in her eyes haunted me. I'd seen this look once before, and I didn't want to remember the time. Yet the more I tried to push the memories away, the more they persisted, rising ever higher, like storm waves on the Great River. At last I could fight them no longer, and let them wash over me in full force:

I see again my mother lying on the bed in her small Institute room. She's drenched in sweat, and tears are flowing down her cheeks.

She'd reached a point of mental despair, where the doctors insisted she must be 'rehabilitated', and her wretched condition now was the result of all he drugs they'd given her.

"Jonah—must tell you the truth." she said in a cracked whisper.

"What truth, Maia?" I was blinking back tears, too, for I was beginning to fear she was dying.

She took several ragged breaths before she spoke again. "You're named for your father," she said in one desperate breath.

I looked up in shock and immediately my eyes went toward Jakol, the only father I'd ever known. He was moving away from us toward the door.

"Jakol knows," she whispered. "He has from the start. Dear patient Jakol. I pray you'll be more like him than your birth-father."

She lapsed into a long silence then, gathering her strength. I felt torn into pieces. Part of me was crying,

'What does this mean? Tell me more!' But another part of me was shrinking back in fear, wanting to run away somewhere and hide.

At last, she took my hand weakly, and spoke again, "Jonah, I was foolish and headstrong when I was young. I hope you don't have to pay for what I've done."

"But, Mother, it must have been long ago."

She smiled a little when I called her Mother. Usually she preferred I use her name, Maia, though I was never sure why. "Yes, it was long ago. But it still haunts me. Though perhaps not much longer."

'No!' I wanted to say. 'You're not going to die!' But the words died in my throat.

"What I did was wrong, even on Rubicon," she whispered. "But I thought I was bold enough and strong enough to handle any situation. I met Jonahkan, Captain of the Nekrae, the Secret Police, when I was very young. He was such a handsome man, very stately with that grey hair at his temples. He was a good friend of my father's, even older than Father was. And I was fascinated with him. He'd bring me gifts when he came to visit Father, and call me his favorite girl-child, or his little shining star.

"I used to pretend I didn't understand the looks he gave me, or the feelings I felt. Then came the secret touches under the table, or behind the door. And soon the danger and fear excited me, and I began to play his deadly game along with him, though I was barely past puberty.

"One day, he came when no one else was home. I knew what the fire in his eyes meant. In fact, I began to burn for him, as well."

Her voice cracked suddenly. "Oh, Jonah, how can I tell you this? And yet you must know the truth now—you must."

By this time my eyes were blinded with hot tears, and my mind was beginning to fill with a red-hot anger. I could find no words to say.

"Yes, there was fire between us that first time," she barely murmured. "Even though I was afraid, I couldn't resist him. You'd think I would have learned then that fire burns. But no! I came whenever he called for me—met him whenever he wished—in whatever secret place he could find. I don't know if I ever thought about the future then. I was too full of pride—to think that a Captain of the Nekrae, the Secret Police of Rubicon, was seeking after me.

"But it wasn't long before I could no longer hide the evidence of you, my Jonah. And then he flew into a rage, shouting terrible things about how he'd never claim you as his own. I felt betrayed and bitter then, and my fire of passion for him turned to hatred. I fled before he could throw me out of his presence, and I never even went back home. Instead I found my way to the secret caves in the hills, where the rebels and exiles hid. I knew if anyone would help me against the Secret Police, they would. That was where dear Jakol took me in, and after you were born, he cared for both of us."

She was fading now. I could see it all too clearly. Her voice was down to the barest whisper. As I wiped the cold sweat from her face, I heard her murmur, "Jakol?"

His voice came from the shadows by the door, "I'm here."

"Jakol is a good man," she gasped, not seeming to care if anyone was listening. "If only *he* were your father. But I see it in your eyes already, Jonah, the fire and power of the Nekrae. I should never have named you for him. But I did it out of spite, since he'd sworn to never claim you.

"And Jakol, who had no reason to, did claim you, terrible name and all. He's always loved us, Jonah," she whispered. "And yet I've never been able to give him my true love in return. I'm too full of anger, fear, and evil. I pray you will somehow escape it."

"My dear Maia," I heard Jakol say.

But at that moment, my mind was full of all the terrible things I'd already done in the Underground. It hit me full force that I truly was the son of my father. I'd just never known it. I was vaguely aware of my mother's body stiffening on the bed and knew she was gone. But even this anguish was smaller than the anger I felt toward myself. I was becoming depraved and evil, and there seemed no way to escape this fate.

Jakol stepped to her side and gently closed her eyes. Then he turned toward me, and I could see his hand reaching out to touch my shoulder, to offer what comfort he could. I've often wondered if my life would have changed if I'd accepted the affection of that generous, loving man. But right then I felt filthy and unclean, totally unworthy of his touch. Before his hand even reached me, I turned and fled the room.

***

The cold waves of memory finally subsided, leaving me lying there chilled and gazing up at the distant stars. As I lay there shivering, I knew I was no better than that Captain of the Nekrae, my unknown and uncaring father. Like him, I'd always taken what I wanted, when I wanted it. Except tonight.

I lay there, hoping my selfish heart was slowly beginning to change. And I vowed that somehow this time, with Martina, it would be different. I'd wait for true love, for her sake—to save her from that anguish I'd seen in her eyes, the same look I'd seen in my mother's eyes when she died.

CHAPTER 6

THE FAR OUTPOST

Even before light dawned the next morning, we found ourselves all alert and anxious to ascend the hill and see what we might find from this new height of observation. It didn't take us long, even in the darkness, to stuff our few belongings back into the bark pack-sacks and start the climb.

The hill was really just a gentle rise and not difficult, even though we'd been walking on such flat ground for so long. But in our excitement, we pushed ourselves, and so were winded when we reached the top.

The sky was the blue-black of pre-dawn, but there was a hint of brightness in the west, behind us. As I turned to look, it struck me how far we'd journeyed since we left The People. The Peaks were gone from sight now—those jagged mountains that had so long dominated our lives. I remembered, standing in that early morning chill, how Jael said they were like the edge of the world, always representing the great obstacle to conquer, the passage on to worlds unknown on the far side.

But now we were far past them, out of their sight, and still bound to the surface of Terres. My heart felt cold and empty, as though we were on the edge of nowhere, with nowhere else to go. But I forced these thoughts from my mind, remembering what Feier told me on that chilly starless night not so long ago.

Colors were beginning to develop in the west now, waves of pink, then orange, and at the center, yellow—fingers of light reaching across the sky. And then at last, the bright edge of Regelian itself, followed soon after by its new twin. As light bathed the plains below us and the air began to warm, I felt my inner self begin to warm slightly, as well.

"What's that?" Martina asked suddenly, pointing off to our right.

"What's what? Where?" I responded.

As I followed her pointing finger, I saw what seemed to be a flash of light from something artificial, perhaps even metallic.

"It looks like the sun shining on Neptune Spire," Jael's voice came excitedly.

"It can't be that. The Spire is gone," I said, still straining my eyes to see. "Besides Terres-City is on the far side of the Peaks, and we can't even see them anymore."

"Unless we've come all the way around the planet," Jael added.

"Don't be silly!" snapped Martina. "We haven't gone *that* far!"

Jael looked hurt. "I'm sorry," he muttered. "You don't have to tell me I'm stupid."

I decided I'd better stay out of their sibling quarrels, though I felt sorry for Jael. It seemed Martina's temper was getting sharper with each passing day. Finally, I decided to try to change the subject.

"The best way to find out, is to just go to it. Come on, let's get going."

They followed me, as we went back down a steeper side of the hill, heading toward the direction where we'd seen the glint of light. We could see nothing now, but I felt sure of the heading.

As the day wore on, and we found nothing unusual, Martina began to get restless, complaining: "Are you sure this is the right direction? We should have seen something by now. Maybe you've gotten off course and missed it."

Her words were biting, and I tried not to let them bother me. But I could tell they were hurting Jael deeply. During one of her sullen silences following an outburst, I drew him closer to me with a hand.

"She'll be all right," I whispered. "It's just that she went through so much back there in the Camp. We all did."

He nodded silently. Then he moved away from me

again, walking behind us, with Feier sitting on his shoulder as he often did. I hoped the telepathic animal gave some encouraging thoughts to him, as we trudged on.

We were walking like this in stony silence as the shadows lengthened into nightfall. As we were topping a slight rise, I began to think it would be good to stop for the night. But just as I opened my mouth to speak, I saw another flash of light, and the others did, too. You couldn't miss it. Right below us in a swale—tinged with orange in the setting sun—was a tower, and on the top a shining sphere. There was a compound surrounding it, with a couple of outbuildings, and here and there the shimmer of a shield.

The others stopped with me, all of us awestruck. I motioned quickly for them to be silent, and we stole quietly out of sight around the edge of the small rise we'd just crossed. Then the questions came fast and furious:

"What is it, Jon?" Jael spoke first.

"Where are we?"

"What should we do?"

Finally a quiet voice came, as I heard Feier saying, 'Listen to Jon. He knows.'

And to my own surprise, I realized I did. It all came back to me from the long drills and training as a Star Corps Cadet. "This is an outpost station," I whispered hoarsely. "They're scattered all across the planet, automated, not manned by Corpsmen, normally. They're just kept for emergency interstellar travel."

"Interstellar?" Martina said, a bit too loudly. Then she whispered, "You mean that tower is a rocket?"

"No," I said. "Just the sphere on top. It's a ship powered by cosmic energy and guided by a Star Corpsman—one who has the power."

"What power?" she asked

"The power to cross the GAP," Jael said quickly. "Don't you remember that Stephen had it? This means we can leave Terres and go to another planet."

She looked confused for a moment. "I guess my mind is still messed up," she sighed. "I sure hope I can get more of my memory back someday."

Jael reached over and took her hand. "You will," he whispered to reassure her.

"But do any of us have the power?" she continued.

"Jon does," replied Jael confidently. "He's firstborn, aren't you?"

"Well, yes," I nodded. "And I used to be a Star Corps Cadet, but I didn't get all the training."

"I know you can do it—like Stephen," Jael said excitedly.

"Well it has been my life-long dream. But I must admit I wasn't a good student in the Corps. You'd be risking your lives with an untried pilot."

"What other choice do we have?" said Martina.

"Do you think we can get into the ship?" Jael asked.

"Even if the outpost isn't manned, there will be an automated guard. If I get the security code, though, maybe I could deactivate the alarm shield."

"How can we get that?" Martina groaned.

'I can.' It was the first time Feier had spoken since the beginning of the conversation. Jael and I fixed our eyes on the little feier-cat, as he seemed to smile up at us. 'I can slip through the shield by staying lower to the ground than any of you. Then I'll find the code in the security program and send it to Jon by telepathy.'

"Are you sure you'll be safe?" Jael asked.

'I'll be careful. Now, wait here.'

He folded his wings very flatly against his back, and they almost disappeared into his fur. Then he crept off into the darkness and left us in uncomfortable silence.

"What's he doing?" Martina asked. "Did he say something to you?"

I nodded, putting a finger to my lips, so she wouldn't talk anymore.

It probably wasn't very long that we sat there, unable to do anything but wait. But it seemed like eternity.

'Jon!' At last the voice came in my mind. 'Here is the code: alpha-theta-ksi. The security entrance is in the east quadrant, to your right. There are only two robot guards, and they will both be deactivated by the code. I'll meet you at the base of the tower on the east.'

Everything went as easily as Feier predicted. I found the entry-gate and punched in the code. Immediately a break appeared in the shield, and we walked in unchallenged. Feier met us at the base of the tower and indicated the necessary code to engage the lift. In what seemed a dream, we were soon stepping through the atmosphere lock into the spherical ship.

The years of studying diagrams and working with simulations at the Academy began to come back to me. I found my mind swinging open like a vast set of doors, to take in all I saw before me.

There at the center of the sphere was the launch console, the reclining chairs all color-coded and arranged around it in a three-dimensional semicircle on the concave floor that was also the walls of the room. Our atmosphere lock entered through a short passage into this central spherical room. Across from this entrance were oval openings at various angles. After launch, each of these would become trapdoor-like openings into private chambers.

I knew that once we were in space, the sphere would begin to rotate, thus generating an artificial gravity field. Down would be toward the outside of the sphere. This control room, being at the center of the sphere, could function under either artificial or planetary gravity.

For a while, I just stood, letting these thoughts flood my mind, and resting my eyes on the metallic sheen of the walls, the colored chairs, the control console. Then I stepped into the room and seated myself in one of those chairs, one with thick padding and a velvety smooth, gold-colored covering--thinking about the G-absorbing qualities of the special materials in this ordinary-seeming chair. Jael was soon seated beside me in the deep blue colored chair, his eyes wide and shining. I motioned for Martina to take the chair with red cushions.

"What about Feier?" Jael asked.

I looked around the spherical room, hoping there was an experimental animal chamber of some kind, and sure enough there was one, lined with bright green cushions, located about sixty degrees from Jael.

"That will be a perfect place for him to be safe during launch," I pointed to it. "After the strong G-forces are past, we can get out of our chairs, and you can let him out again."

Jael picked up his feier-cat tenderly and sealed him into the little launch chamber.

"Martina," I went on, "Put your hand over those sensors at the atmosphere lock, until the digital counters read 'ten'. That will seal the lock. Then secure our packs in one of the private rooms on our present level."

"How do I secure them?"

"There should be a small chamber, like a closet—put the gear in there as tightly as you can, just so it doesn't bounce around too much. Jael will help you."

I could tell from their short replies and quickness to follow my orders they were in awe of our new situation.

Hopefully I'd live up to their confidence in my ability to handle all this. I wasn't sure I had that much confidence in myself.

While they were doing these chores, I studied the controls. At the warmth of my body heat, the sensors initiated the power, and multicolored readings appeared. In the center of the panel was a large blank area that would become a three-dimensional display of our spatial location once we were in space. The detail of the display would depend on my strength in using the power. The more I knew about a given sector, and the greater my perception, the better database we'd have from which to navigate. But right now, as a completely untried novice and on the surface of a planet for which I knew no coordinates in space, I was flying completely blind.

By this time, the others completed stowing the gear and strapped themselves into their chairs. A low hum was beginning to fill the air around us, as the ship's propulsion system became activated by my presence at the controls. I placed my hands on the arms of the gold-colored navigation chair and felt the warm red glow as my heat and flesh patterns were imprinted. I was now fully recognized as the pilot of this ship.

Now all I had to do was engage my mental powers, close my eyes, and cross the GAP, just as I'd practiced with myself in the City. But this time, I would be linked with the cosmic power crystals of the ship, and we'd be leaping off the surface of the planet into some unknown location in space.

Jael and Martina looked at me in wide-eyed anticipation, and I just nodded to them. How could I tell them the possibilities of what we faced? I needed more data than I had. I hadn't been trained in the initial navigation of the new Terran sky, which changed drastically with the coming of the double-star, when our new sun had dragged us across unknown space. This ship hadn't been reprogrammed either, I could tell. Perhaps the City no longer existed, so there was no one to reprogram. We had no way of knowing.

In my mind, I weighed the odds of our making this first crossing successfully. If I moved us to the exact coordinates of one of Terres' moons, or of a nearby planet, we would meet our end right there, encased in solid rock. Or there was the possibility of our being scorched to a crisp if I put us too close to one of our twin suns. But what other choice did I have?

'After all,' I told myself, just to get up my nerve. 'They do call it space, don't they? That means ninety-nine percent of the coordinates out there are empty space. Odds are ninety-nine to one. All right, not too bad.'

I fastened the straps and pressed my back into the moldable padding of the pilot's chair.

"Okay, everybody. Keep your body in contact with the cushion for its full length. This will enable you to endure the G-forces. Are you ready?"

"Yes, Jon," Jael spoke first.

"Me, too."

"Here goes."

I closed my eyes, half-praying in the back of my mind to whatever spirit might hear me. The pressure built, and I could feel heat rising around us. My hands tingled where they touched the glowing arms of the chair. The pressure increased, and I concentrated on keeping it steady and even. There was no sound, and only a vague sensation of movement. I was the only one of us who could feel this movement, I knew, for I was the only firstborn. Then came the slightest hint of a spinning sensation, telling me we'd left Terres' gravity, and the ship had initiated its own gravitational field.

All these feelings came in a flash, much faster than I can even tell them. They were identical to the feelings I had as a boy leaving Rubicon on that huge starship. For an instant, I felt as if I were back in time, in the hull of the ship with my parents beside me. Perhaps—as I crossed time in the GAP—I *was* with them again, in a sense. I almost thought I could see their faces.

Then I opened my eyes, and saw other faces looking at me—Jael and Martina, eyes bright with wonder and fear.

"You can unstrap yourselves now," I smiled. "We're in space."

CHAPTER 7

THE HEAVENS ARE TELLING

With a touch of my hand on the panel, I activated the display. A sphere of vague brownish tinge dominated the view, but it was getting visibly smaller as we watched. Jael and Martina just stared at it, speechless.

At last Jael asked, "Is that really Terres?"

"It's a projection of it," I smiled.

"But is it really that big—I mean that small—out there?"

"Sure is, Little Brother. We're leaving it behind."

"Oh."

His voice tapered off and disappeared in wonder. Then he rose carefully, almost floating in the lesser gravity of the ship.

"Wow!" he cried. "I feel like I'm flying or like I'm under water."

"It's just the lower gravity. You'll get used to it."

As I spoke to him, I found my eyes resting on Martina. Her green eyes were wide, and they looked so beautiful that way. I wanted to reach over and take her hand, or touch her cheek, but knew I shouldn't. So, I released myself from my chair and moved slowly over to Jael, patting him on the back instead.

"Here, I'll help you get Feier out. Now, since your chair is blue, you get to take the trap door that's blue for your sleeping quarters. Martina's will be the red one, and mine is gold. I smiled over at her as I spoke and was pleased when her eyes smiled back at me.

Still holding Feier, Jael stood for a moment, seemingly uncertain.

"Jon?"

"Yes, Jael?"

"When will we get there?"

"Get where?"

"Where we're going." Then his face began to flush in confusion. "I mean—when will we get somewhere—or where will we be when we get somewhere—or…"

He tried to smile, and I couldn't help but chuckle.

"My mind is boggled, too," I said, rubbing his head. "When we get somewhere, wherever that is, then we'll know where we are."

Now he was smiling, and I could almost feel his eyes shining at me. "I'm sure glad you're firstborn, Jon," he said. "And we can voyage to the stars."

"I am, too," I smiled. And at that moment, more than any other in my life, I truly was glad I had the power to cross the GAP. I felt as though I'd found my calling, at last.

"Where *are* we going, Jon?" Martina asked.

There was a challenging tone in her voice, and I wanted to give a firm answer, but there just wasn't enough data yet.

"Don't you have *any* idea?" she added.

"Not yet," I tried to smile. "I don't have any idea what's out there. Do you?"

"How could I?" she retorted.

"Hey, don't get mad," Jael put in.

"Jael's right," I nodded. "Anger won't do any good. Since the coming of the double-star, I've lost all my bearings, Martina. We've been taken to a new quadrant of space. Once we've located a few more known systems, though, I can try to pentabulate."

"Pentabulate? What's that?" Jael asked.

"Well, it means to get some coordinates on the viewer—to put it simply."

"In school, they taught us to triangulate, using the three dimensions of space," said Martina. "Is it like that?"

I nodded. "It's similar, except that pentabulation uses five dimensions—time and the GAP, besides the three dimensions of space."

"And you can do that because you're firstborn, right?" said Jael.

"That gives me the potential, but I still have a lot to learn. It takes time and practice, just like learning anything else. I'll do my best, but you'll just have to bear with me while I'm learning." Even as I said these words, I thought, 'How ironic to hear myself saying the words my instructors in Star Corps used to tell me. I was way too restless and impulsive then.'

They were both nodding, and Martina seemed to smile at me for an instant. Or was it only my imagination?

"Hey, what's that?" Jael asked suddenly, pointing in excitement at the viewer in front of me.

Turning to follow his gesture, we saw a shining cloud slowly moving into the viewer from the left perimeter. Gradually it grew in size, as it moved toward the middle of the projection. Soon the cloudy whiteness began to shine with different colors, and occasional bright flashes stabbed at our eyes.

"What is it, Jon?" Martina asked.

"It looks like a nebula—a large group of stars and gas molecules," I said.

"Will it swallow us up?" asked Jael, sounding fearful.

"I don't think there's any danger. It's so huge that it looks closer than it is. We're really hundreds of kilometers from it."

"Really?"

"Well, as best as I can calculate without any star charts."

"How come we can see it?" Martina asked. "I thought you controlled this projection viewer with your mind."

"I just augment it with what knowledge I have of the sector we're in. The viewer shows what's in scanner-sight automatically. I can add what's out of sight if I have good charts. Hopefully someday, we'll have a more complete view."

By now the whole screen was filled with the nebula, and the flashes were beginning to seem blinding.

"Are you sure we're safe, Jon?"

"I'm beginning to wonder, Martina. I don't want to get lost in that maze of stars either. Hold on while I cross to some new coordinates."

Placing my hands on the imprinted controls, I closed my eyes, trying to sense which GAP-crossing would move us back into open space. My powers were still limited, and time was short, so I had to take a quick jump without any real bearings. I felt the ship shudder for an instant and opened my eyes to watch the viewer. The nebula moved rapidly out of sight in a smooth, creamy stream.

"Wow, it seemed like the nebula moved instead of us," Jael cried in surprise.

"I didn't feel us move either," added Martina.

"That's normal from what I've been taught. I'm the only one here who will actually feel the crossing."

"Unless Feier is firstborn. Then he will, won't he?" said Jael.

I chuckled. "I don't know if the power applies to feier-cats."

"Well, after all this excitement, I'm hungry," he added.

"Me too," nodded Martina. "And I'm tired of berry-leather. Do they store any food on these things?"

"They should," I said.

So, we all searched the storage areas around the spherical room, bringing out any packets of preserved food we could find.

"They all look good still," I noted, as we counted our find. "About fifty packets, huh? Well, hopefully that will last us until we can find an inhabited system." I tried to sound hopeful to the others. but I had my doubts about my ability to meet this tight schedule. After all, what were the odds of our just stumbling onto an inhabited system just by wandering aimlessly in uncharted space? I didn't even want to calculate it.

"For now, let's each pick one packet and stow the rest," I said as cheerfully as I could. "We should be careful to conserve what food we have."

Soon I occupied them with learning to use the warming console. Then we began sampling the supposed delicacies of space travel.

"Well, what do you think?" I asked between mouthfuls. "Beats berry-leather, huh?" I winked at Jael.

"Sure does."

"This Sirian soup isn't too bad," said Martina. "Want a taste?"

"Sure, I'll trade you a bite of Regelian gulias," I smiled.

"We'd better save some for Feier," said Jael. "I didn't find any animal food."

"Maybe when we restock we'll find some," I said.

"How do we get more food, anyway?" asked Martina. "Can we just go to any planet and ask for it?"

"I was afraid you'd ask that question." I tried to laugh, but some Regelian gulias caught in my throat. Once I'd recovered from choking, I tried again to give some light-hearted answer, but Martina cut in before I could speak:

"No really, Jon. Can we get more food?"

"I'm sure we'll find a way when we get to a planet. We'll just have to see what sort of culture they have before we'll know how to deal with them."

"*If* we get to somewhere," she said softly.

Jael was silent as we talked, and I saw him pull out his ragged little pamphlet of words from some ancient book. I'd forgotten that little booklet of his with its 'Words to Remember.' Now suddenly, the sight of it brought back memories of the last time I saw it, in a cold, dark cave in the Wilds of Terres.

"So you still have your little book, Jael."

"Just this pamphlet of sayings from The Book."

"You remember that night in the cave when you found my song in there?"

He nodded slowly.

"You told me our help comes from the Lord."

"Yes, it's right here," he began to read. "'My help comes from the Lord, who made Heaven and Earth'."

"Who is this Lord?" asked Martina.

"Don't you remember anything Stephen taught us?" Jael looked at his sister in a puzzled way.

She shook her head. "Maybe it will come back—if I find my memories."

"I don't know who this Lord is either," I said softly. "I want to keep searching."

Following Jael's gaze to the viewer, I saw a new star system appearing. Off to the right was a small cluster of suns all circling each other. On the left, and moving toward the center, was a single huge red star, and farther back other smaller, more distant points of light.

"This Lord must be terribly great if he really made the whole Universe," Jael breathed in awe. "Just look at all those stars. It's so beautiful."

"And this is only a small corner of one galaxy," I added. "There's so much more out there than we can even imagine."

"We sure could get lost out there-" Martina began.

"But if we're looking for the Lord of the Universe, he must be in the Universe he made, somewhere," I interrupted.

"Perhaps," she sighed.

"Listen," Jael cried excitedly. "Here are some words Stephen once told me. They're in The Book, too. 'The heavens are telling the glory of God, and the earth shows his handiwork'."

We all gazed at the viewer in silence for a few moments, each feeling in his own heart the deep meaning of those words.

"He's out there somewhere all right," I whispered at last. "We'll find him."

No one replied, but I hadn't really expected them to. Silence settled around us again, as the ship gradually shifted to the edge of the coordinates. Soon I'd have to cross the GAP again, hoping to find an inhabited system. Then Martina's voice interrupted my thoughts:

"When did Stephen tell you that, Jael?"

"You mean those words? One night when we were watching the stars out my window. I'd just learned to read. It seems so long ago now." His voice was wavering, and I saw tears shining in his eyes.

"I sure miss Stephen," Martina whispered.

"Me too, Sis."

"Do you think he knew where to find this Lord of the Universe?"

I felt myself wanting to speak but bit my lip instead. I could sense how dear this older brother was to them, and I didn't want to intrude. Suddenly I realized that no matter how much I'd like to take Stephen's place in their affections, I never could. No person can ever replace another. So, I sat in silence as their sad voices continued.

"I don't know if Stephen knew where this Lord was," Jael was saying. "But I like to think perhaps he's with him now."

"With the Lord of the Universe? How?"

"I don't know, Martina. It's just a feeling I have, that's all. Say, do you think we could look for Darien? He must be out in this Galaxy somewhere."

"If only we could find him," she sighed. "Perhaps that would help fill this emptiness."

I felt their eyes turn to me and looked up.

"What do you think, Jon?" she asked.

"About finding your other brother?"

"Yes—Darien. He was just two standard years younger than Stephen. He joined the Inland Raiders after Stephen died."

"Well, as long as we're searching anyway, who knows if we might stumble onto some Inland Raiders, too." I really didn't think the odds of this were even measurable but didn't want to tell them this.

"We must never give up," said Jael softly. "That's what you taught me on top of that icy ridge in the Wilds."

These words seemed to give me a glimmer of hope. "Yes, I guess I did," I smiled slowly.

Feier suddenly rose from a nap and jumped into Jael's arms. 'Remember there's always hope,' he said.

"Have you been sleeping or listening, Feier?" I asked.

'Both,' he replied.

"Did Feier say something to you?" Martina asked. "I can't hear him at all."

"It's okay, Sis. Maybe as your memories return, you'll be able to hear him."

"I sure hope so," she shrugged. "I don't like feeling left out."

I nodded to both of them and said, "So we'll search as long as we have life."

"For a better place to live," Jael added.

"And for Darien." said Martina.

'Don't forget the Lord of the Universe,' Feier said in my mind.

"That's right," said Jael, so I knew he'd heard Feier too.

After this, we all lapsed into a long silence. We still talked about everyday things like the food we were eating, and occasionally a new wonder of the Galaxy would appear on the viewer for us to marvel at, like a blazing blue star, or a new cluster. Once we even got close enough to a dim red star to see a few circling planets. But there was never any response to our contact signals.

Still, we all kept silent about our hopes and fears after that long talk. Perhaps we thought we'd bring ourselves bad luck if we talked too much about it. Or perhaps we realized, wisely I think now, that we'd just get our hopes too high.

Sometime during this period, Jael found a Star Corps uniform stowed in the back of one of the sleeping room closets. I was elated to see it, yet almost ashamed I hadn't thought to look for it myself. I realized suddenly that we had to come up with a plausible way to explain ourselves to the authorities, when we finally reached somewhere.

"Well, how does it look?" I asked the others, once I had it on.

"Very official," Martina smiled.

'A bit baggy,' said Feier.

"Well, I haven't exactly been eating a lot lately," I shrugged. I'd been making sure everyone else got enough before I took any, especially the last couple of weeks. "I hope I look official enough to convince some tough officials I have a right to pilot this ship," I quickly added, to change the subject.

"That's right!" Jael said.

"Why hadn't I thought of that?" Martina added.

'I thought of it,' Feier said in my mind.

"You guys haven't found any other clothes, have you?" I asked.

"No," she replied. "We don't look very official in these worn bark-clothes, either."

'Maybe you could say we're Inland Raiders on a secret mission,' Feier said.

"Sounds good," I nodded. "Did you guys hear that?"

Jael nodded, but Martina was shaking her head. "For some reason, only you two can hear Feier."

"He said, we could try to convince them you're Inland Raiders," I said quickly. "I think it's the best we can do for now. We won't know if it works until we try it on someone."

I tried to sound optimistic, hoping to hide my doubts and fears from them. Each time we crossed a GAP, the signal we devised was transmitted:

"Star Corps T-067 Shuttle Craft, seeking refueling stop. Please acknowledge."

Before long, our food stores were getting dangerously low, and I began crossing the GAP more frequently and in more hazardous areas, in hopes of finding something. 'If only I had a star chart,' I thought to myself over and over. Sometimes Feier would turn and look at me, and I knew he was reading my thoughts.

Then as we were eating almost our last meal packets, there came the most welcome sound I think I've ever heard—the sharp two-tone indicating incoming communication:

"Star Corps Shuttle Craft T-067, this is Fatina Base Station. What are your needs? Over."

CHAPTER 8

FATINA

I grabbed the communicator. "Fatina Base Station, this is T-067, do you read?"

"Affirmative."

"Request permission to take on new stores."

"What is your mission, T-067?"

"Galactic Rebel suppression," I said, hoping my voice sounded even and authoritative. "Special mission."

There was a long silence then, and my heart began to pound loudly. Had I messed up already? I didn't even know if we were near a Galactic War sector.

"You're a bit off course, aren't you?" the voice returned at last.

"Affirmative. We had some problems."

"We'll expect a full report when you arrive. Locking your ship in now."

I felt the gentle shift in the ship as their tractor beam locked us into its pull. This would guide our ship to the dock site where the officials of Fatina wanted us. We couldn't turn back now.

As we drew closer to the planet, I could see it was very densely populated. The majority of the planet's surface appeared to be one huge city, making Terres-City look like a village in comparison. Everything we'd seen and heard so far confirmed my suspicions this was a part of the Galactic System like Terres. This was good since they would speak our language, and it was our best chance of finding supplies for our Star Corps vessel. But I also knew there were risks. Our chances of convincing the officials our rag-tag crew was on a Star Corps mission were low. In fact, we might have lost our credibility already.

Soon we'd entered the atmosphere of Fatina, and pinkish-white clouds obscured all view of the planet's surface. In fact, we'd entered a section of cloud so thick I barely saw the Space Port until we were right in front of the yawning port doors. The beam drew us steadily through that dark opening, and as soon as our craft was past the doors, I heard them slide firmly shut.

Jael and Martina sat in silence after the first communi-cation, for I motioned for them not to speak. I could tell by their eyes, though, they sensed our peril as much as I did.

"We must try to stay together," I said softly, at last breaking the silence. I had to risk that little bit of commu-nication, even if we were being monitored. "Let me do the talking."

These words were barely out of my mouth, when I heard the hiss of the airlock. We managed to get out of our chairs, and Jael grabbed Feier, just as three uniformed men entered. One had a gleaming official insignia on his shoulder, and the others appeared to be guards.

"Shir Kanah," said the official, saluting sharply.

I saluted back, trying not to remember how I was criticized for my salute at the Academy. I wasn't sure what to say either, but he seemed to have given a name, so I gave the most official-sounding one I could, "Jonahkan."

"You will come with us," he snapped.

I motioned for the others to follow me, hoping he meant all of us. The official made no motion to stop them, so we all started toward the airlock.

Doors hissed open before us, and closed sharply behind us, as we were led through a maze of hallways. My mind was flying, desperately trying to memorize the path we were taking, so I could get us back to the ship.

But the farther we went, the more disoriented I became, and knew they were probably doing this on purpose. Old resentments began to rise within me—ones I'd felt at the Star Corps Academy—anger at the rigidity of the Galactic System and frustration at the purposely confusing maze of rooms and corridors. The old familiar ache in my head returned, caused by the bright lights, shining walls, and patterned floors.

At last, we stopped in a small cubicle containing four

chairs and a square table. Without a word, Shir Kanah and his companions stepped back out the single door and left us alone. As the door hissed ominously closed, I had a feeling those guards were just outside.

"Why do I suddenly feel like we're in prison?" asked Martina.

I put my finger to my lips quickly, knowing there would be listening sensors in this room. There was nothing we could do now but hope this was part of the normal procedure on this planet. We sat in silence for what seemed like hours. It was probably only a matter of minutes, but with no sounds except Feier's humming, the seconds stretched toward eternity.

Then I heard Feier's voice in my mind. Of course, I could talk to him silently.

'Do you have a plan, Jon?'

'Well, I had one,' I thought back to him. 'But it may have gone wrong already. I need more information about this place. Somehow, we have to get supplies and get back to our ship, but I'm all turned around now. I wonder if I made a big mistake in coming here at all.'

'But what other choice was there?' he asked.

'None I could see, except to run out of food and starve in space.'

'Then keep your courage, Jon. There must be a purpose in this situation.'

'I hope you're right.'

At last the door hissed open again, and another official entered with one of the guards. On his forehead was the badge of a Questioner. Now I was certain of what I'd feared. This was *not* routine—we were under suspicion.

This first questioning wasn't long, but we didn't do very well.

"So, you say you're on a special Star Corps mission?" the Questioner asked, looking directly at Martina.

This disconcerted me, for I knew he was working on our weakest link.

"Yes," she nodded.

"And what is your destination?"

"We need to find the Inland Raiders," she blurted out.

The Questioner raised his eyebrows at this. Already she'd said too much. I had no choice but to try to intervene, "What she means, sir," I said quickly, "Is that these three, my passengers, are carrying a highly secret message to an Inland Raider contingent."

"A search and destroy message, perhaps?" he smiled wickedly.

From this I knew instantly he thought we were Rebels ourselves, and not Inland Raider messengers at all.

"And what is he?" he smirked, pointing to Feier, "The secret message?"

"He bears the message," I said, trying to keep my confidence up.

Apparently, the Questioner heard enough to convince him, though, for he rose from his chair abruptly. "We will question further," he said. Then he and the guard were gone.

My throat was very tight as I looked at the others. Jael's eyes were wide, and I wasn't sure he fully understood our situation. But Martina seemed to. She was staring at her hands as they lay spread on the table.

"Can we talk yet?" whispered Jael.

"It probably won't hurt anything now," I shrugged.

"What are they going to do with us?" muttered Martina.

"They think we're Rebels who stole a Star Corps ship," I whispered hoarsely.

"But we aren't Rebels," cried Jael.

"What else would you call us?" I mumbled.

"Refugees," said Martina. "Refugees from-"

"Sh!" I said before she could say too much of where we came from. But then I realized they could tell that from our ship's call number. I began to wonder if they knew anything about the destruction of Terres-City. Perhaps we *could* convince them we were refugees.

As these thoughts were darting through my mind, Jael whispered, "Do you think we might find the Lord of the Universe in this place? It seems to be a huge great city, a place where a really powerful being might rule."

"I don't know," I shrugged. "I know he must be powerful to rule the Universe, but I'm not sure he would rule from a System planet."

"Maybe he's not really a person," said Martina. "Maybe he's a spirit—like the Great Spirit of the People—and moves in another realm."

We both stared at her. Jael seemed to be weighing her words carefully, and with a light of revelation in his eyes. But after what I'd seen of the dreadful powers of the Great Spirit of the People and his demons, I hoped fervently the Lord of the Universe was not like him. This thought scared me even more than the almost certain captivity we were facing at that moment on Fatina.

Just as I was about to express some of this, the door hissed sharply open, and there stood the guard who'd come with the Questioner. His face seemed almost to be made of stone, and his eyes had a steely glint. Here was a man who could do very unpleasant tasks, it seemed.

"You," he said gruffly, pointing at me, "Come with me."

He left no opening to question. I could only give the others a glance and hope they'd still be here when I got back—if I got back.

The guard led me down several more hallways in the maze, just until I was disoriented again. At each turn, I expected him to turn into one of the questioning cells where the Electronic Questioner would do its work of drawing all thoughts from my mind. But suddenly, we turned into a strange, dimly-lit hallway. I was puzzled, but thankful for the momentary rest for my glare-weary eyes.

"Turn here," he hissed in my ear, and guided me toward an unmarked door. Suddenly we were in a storage area of some sort, and my puzzlement increased. His face of stone seemed to have melted in the dim light, and his eyes lost their glint. Still, I wasn't at all prepared for his next words:

"Long live the King," he whispered, with great feeling in his voice. "I can help you escape, but you must do exactly as I say. I, too, am one with your cause."

"My cause?" I said without thinking. 'Perhaps he's testing my loyalty,' I thought.

But apparently, he thought I was testing him, for he straightened and replied with great respect in his voice, "May our Lord overcome the false usurper."

I nodded at him, pretending I understood. If he was going to help us, this was all that mattered at this point.

"You must go to Pyrrhia and seek Gur-Bu'tah," he continued. "I'm told it's the closest place which can give you any guidance in your search for the Lord of the Universe."

My mind began running on two tracks. So, he'd heard our words about the Lord of the Universe. Evidently this had something to do with his cause, and his willingness to help us. Yet most of my mind was on more urgent matters at the moment.

"How do we get to Pyrrhia?" I asked quickly. "We have no star charts."

"None at all?" He seemed astounded.

"No, we don't even know what sector we're in."

"Then you merely stumbled onto Fatina by chance? And I of all the force am assigned to guard you?" his voice was full of awe. "The hand of the Lord must be in this."

"Is there no other help on Fatina then?"

"There are only a few of us, a mere handful on this huge planet. We're too weak for much action. There's no Lord and King here—only the Mind rules, the great, unfeeling, cold Mind. And it feeds on the minds of such as you. We must get back to the others quickly before the Questioner sends for them."

As he talked, he was stuffing some food packets into a shoulder bag. "This will get you to Pyrrhia. Ah, and here's a partial star chart program." He pulled a tiny disc from one of the shelves over our heads. "You're firstborn, aren't you?"

"Oh yes. Otherwise we couldn't have gotten here at all."

"Someone great is guiding you," he whispered. "Now take this bag. We have little time."

He went out the door first, and then motioned for me

to follow. In a very short time, we were back at the cubicle with the others. Evidently, he took a much less circuitous route this time.

As soon as I entered, Jael ran up and threw his arms around me, fear filling his eyes. I put my finger to his lips and motioned for them to be silent. Then I looked at the guard. That stony look was back on his face, but it had new meaning for me. Now I knew it was his disguise, to hide his true feelings from prying eyes.

He didn't speak but motioned to the corners where listening sensors must be planted. Again, he stepped out first and led us through another maze of hallways. With every step my ears pounded harder. At any moment I expected us to be discovered. Yet, some power beyond us must have been protecting us, for we met no one until we came to the deck-port where our ship was housed.

"Halt! Restricted area!" a voice suddenly boomed.

Our guard quickly activated the door ahead of us. "Your ship is in there. Go quickly, and with God the Lord."

He pushed us through the door, and as it closed again, we saw a flash of blinding light and heard a terrible scream.

"Run!" I cried, heading for the ship. "Or we'll be next!"

Somehow, we managed to clamber through the airlock and get it sealed. The instant our bodies touched the chairs I put my hands on the console panel, activating it. Fortunately, it responded quickly since my pattern was already imprinted. I had no time to consult the Star Chart, but just threw us across the first GAP I could think of, an intermediate passage into what I hoped was open space.

The ship began to vibrate violently. With a sinking heart I realized we were probably still locked into a tractor beam. I increased my concentration on open space. A hot white light split right through my mind, and I felt a searing pain. My mind began to waver, and then I saw myself on the brink of some vast black pit. By some force of will power I didn't even know I possessed, I pulled myself back from the edge. Then a warm grayness engulfed me from behind. I'd lost control. Some other power was taking me wherever it willed.

***

"Jon? Are you, all right?" The voice sounded like it was coming a great distance down a tunnel. I tried to climb slowly toward the pinpoint of light above me. At last, the light framed Martina's face. Dear Martina. Had I failed her?

"Sorry," I heard my voice murmur. "I tried as hard as I could. They were too strong."

"It's all right, Jon," she whispered. "We made it. We escaped."

Now my vision widened to include Jael. "We did?" I asked incredulously. "But I lost control. Some other power took over."

"Well, it wasn't them," said Jael.

'We're safe,' Feier added. 'No pursuers in sight.'

I was speechless. Some other power working for us? Perhaps there was some hope in the Universe after all.

'Just like I told you,' Feier said.

CHAPTER 9

THE PASSIVE PLANET

As soon as I felt strong enough to focus on things, I asked Martina to bring me the Star Chart. It wasn't actually a map on paper, as you'd be used to in your time. Instead it was a series of numbers and coordinates to be fed into the ship's control system. This gave us some orientation for the first time in our voyage. The figures which glowed on the control panel told me that we were about halfway between Fatina and Pyrrhia.

Again, I wondered about this force which had literally pulled us off Fatina. Not only had it brought us out of the power of their tractor beam, but it took us in the direction we wanted to go. I hadn't known the headings when I took the controls, but here we were on that very course.

At this thought, I sat in awe for a few minutes. The tiny lighted numbers coincided with the visual display. We were located at last, and now I could really be a star pilot, just like I always dreamed.

Yet so much was happening which was beyond my

own power. What was that overwhelming force I'd felt as we left Fatina? It obviously wasn't from there, and yet it was here to help in our time of desperate need. The very thought of something so powerful, and apparently knowledgeable, boggled my mind.

"Are we still lost?" Martina asked, interrupting my thoughts.

"Uhh--" I literally had to pull my mind back into the present, and the effort required surprised me. "No, I think I have our location coordinated now."

"Really?" came Jael's excited voice. "Where are we?"

"About halfway between Fatina and a place called Pyrrhia."

"Pyrrhia? What's that?" asked Martina.

"I hope it's not another System planet where they'll capture us as Rebels again," sighed Jael.

"Yes," she nodded, and added very softly, "It's like we have nowhere we can be safe—ever again-"

Her voice suddenly broke, and I wanted to take her in my arms right then and comfort her. But I'd made a promise to her that I'd wait for her to be ready, so I just tried to comfort her with my voice.

"I know. I feel the same deep inside. But there is hope. I really believe that. Some great force beyond ourselves helped us escape Fatina. And the guard, our nameless friend, told me we should seek someone on Pyrrhia—someone called Gur-Bu'tah."

"What a strange name," mused Jael.

"I think we should see if we can find him," I said. "How about you guys?"

"We don't have anywhere else to go, do we?" shrugged Martina.

I could tell by the attempted casual tone in her voice she'd put the wall between us back up again.

"All right, then," I said. "Secure yourselves and we'll cross the GAP to Pyrrhia."

This was the first GAP I'd crossed using coordinates, the first time I really knew what I was doing. In less time than it takes to tell, our viewer was displaying a small yellow sun with a single planet circling it.

'What a small system,' I said to myself. 'But the data shows it's Pyrrhia.'

The others were watching the viewer in silence, but Feier heard my thoughts, 'Do you think it's safe, Jon? We have only the guard's word to go on.'

'I'll be more careful this time,' I said in my mind. 'I'll avoid spaceports and tractor beams. I think I can set us in an unpopulated area.'

We were now in range to get magnified views of the planet's surface. It wasn't very densely populated, especially compared to Fatina. Using this visual data, I made a short crossing, and in that instant the ship settled gently onto the surface of the lone planet Pyrrhia. My sensors immediately registered an atmosphere safe for humans.

"Looks good so far," I said to the faces looking to me for the next move. "Let's see what's out there."

As we gingerly climbed out of the ship, a gentle warm breeze wafted over us. The area we'd landed in was a clearing surrounded by a strange forest of giant herbs. The stalks were tall and thick, but not at all woody. It was hard to believe they were standing so tall, high above our heads, without bending under their own weight.

Drawing away from the ship into this quiet cool forest, I felt a sense of peace. After walking a short distance under the herbs, we came to a much larger opening. Before us stretched a vast open plain, bright yellow in color. A wall of heat seemed to hit us in the face.

"Whew! What a sudden change," said Jael.

We stopped then at the edge of the plain, shading our eyes to see what was beyond in the shimmering heat.

"Looks like a village of some sort out there," I said.

"Yes, and perhaps some peaks in the far distance," he added.

"More peaks at the edge of the world, eh Jael?"

He smiled up at me. "Well, perhaps they are."

"Is it safe to leave the ship out here?" asked Martina. "We sure don't want to lose it."

"We'll have to leave it, if we want to find this Gur-Bu'tah," I said. "Unless you have some other plan."

I hadn't meant to sound sharp with her, but she took it that way. "No!" she snapped. "I don't!"

Before I really realized what I was doing, I'd put my hand on her shoulder. Immediately she jerked away.

"Just keep your hands to yourself! I've already told you that!" She turned on her heel and headed toward the ship. "I'll get the gear, if you insist on looking for this Gur—whoever he is."

She disappeared back into the greenery before I could apologize. Then I felt a small hand in mine and looked down to see tears glistening in Jael's eyes.

"She'll be all right," I tried to reassure him. "She still has to recover from all she went through with the Redlarks."

"And before that in the City, in the Underground."

I didn't really know much of what happened to Martina in the Underground, except that she'd been Jason's woman. There must have been something wrong, which caused her to take the same radical step I had, disconnecting from all she knew to join the Redlarks.

Just then Feier appeared at our feet.

"Where have you been?" I asked him.

'Getting myself some fresh food,' he replied. 'It's been a long time.'

"Fresh food sounds good to me, too," said Jael. "I'm tired of those food packets."

"What?" I teased. "I thought Sirian soup was your favorite."

"It used to be," he smiled. "Say, Jon?"

"What?"

"Isn't there some kind of force shield you can put around the ship, so it will be safe while we're gone?"

"You're right, there should be." I jumped up. "Why didn't I think of that?"

"Seeing Feier reminded me," he shrugged. "I remembered how he got us through the shield at the Outpost."

I was already starting back to the ship as he finished. "Come on!" I called over my shoulder.

We found Martina pulling the last of our packs through the airlock.

"Jon thinks he can put a shield around the ship," Jael called to her.

I was glad to see her face brighten at his voice. "That's a great idea!"

As soon as we got our gear, including a little sensor pack for Feier, I told them to stand clear, while I went back into the ship to check for a shield activator. Sure enough, there was one, complete with a delay timer. So I set this for fifty seconds, just enough time to get myself through the airlock, and I made sure I put a portable shield deactivator in my pack for future use.

Just as I reached the others, a shimmering began around the ship. I was especially pleased to see it even caused the outline of the ship to blur and blend into the surrounding scenery. It wasn't quite invisible, but someone would really have to search carefully to find it.

We didn't say much as we started off for the yellow plain and the village we'd seen in the distance. Our minds were filled with hopes and fears as we again set off into the unknown, hoping against hope that we'd find the better life we were seeking.

When we neared the village, we discovered it was much larger than expected. The shimmering heat of the plain, and the distance, made its sprawling buildings of buff stone look like mere huts. But the closer we got, the more it looked like a real city with multistory buildings.

The heat was scorching, but at least it lacked the oppressive feeling of humidity. Soon we were passing through an ancient-looking gate in a stone wall. There were no guards at the gate, which was encouraging. The wall was in such poor condition, guards would have been of little defensive help anyway.

As we walked down the cobblestone streets, a few people passed us, but none seemed to pay us any heed. Most of them wore long, loose robes of white or pale colors. Some carried baskets slung over their shoulders, laden with fruit and greens. One small handcart passed us, creaking plaintively.

The buildings which appeared to be single large dwellings now turned out to be groups of small houses huddled together, some actually on top of each other, a jumble of doorways and small windows. All were of the same buff-colored stone, roughly cut and piled in blocks, apparently without any mortar.

We were nearing what appeared to be a sort of town square when someone finally took notice of us and approached.

"Peace be to you," he said, bowing to us.

It was an unexpected greeting, and our first assurance we weren't on a System planet.

"What do you seek?" he continued, his face not really smiling or frowning.

I was so mystified by the blank passive look on his face that for a moment I couldn't respond to his question.

"Uh—we're looking for Gur-Bu'tah," I managed to stutter.

"Ah, the Master. Yes, of course." He didn't seem at all surprised at our request. "I will take you."

Soon we were standing in front of one of those small stone buildings. But it was no different from any of the others, and we all found ourselves glancing at each other. Could "The Master" really be in such an ordinary place?

Just as I turned to ask our guide if he was sure this was the right place, the door opened before us, and there stood a tall man with a long flowing beard of the purest white I've ever seen. The hair cascading over his shoulders matched exactly and merged with the beard, so his face seemed to float in a sea of white.

"Peace to you, Qan'tah," he nodded to our guide. "More wanderers, I see. Thank you."

Our guide merely nodded and walked away without a word.

Then the bearded man turned to us, showing no surprise at all.

"You are seekers," he said simply. "Come in, and we will share where we've been."

***

Thus began our life on Pyrrhia, the most peaceful time of our lives. We were given a house of our own, one of the little stone places—two rooms, each with a window. Jael and I offered Martina the smaller back room to herself, and she seemed to like the idea. She even smiled at me for a few seconds, but this almost made it harder for me. How I wished she'd said she would rather have a room with me, like when she was my Consort in the Redlark Camp.

Each day, we went into the fields near the city to till and gather our own food. There was no meat consumed here, only plants and vegetables. Often in the beginning, Gur-Bu'tah himself would accompany us, talking about everything around us and telling us what he called the 'Truths of the Universe.'

"All you see is God," he told us. "Everything is God, and God is everything. God isn't just *in* the Universe, he *is* the Universe. You have no more need to search the galaxies for him. He's all around you. Just look within yourself."

This was a wonder to us, for we'd each searched so long in our lives. It was hard to believe we had the answer within ourselves all along. Now we hoped we'd found our answer at last.

In the evenings Gur-Bu'tah would sit with us in his doorway, teaching us to meditate.

"To truly look within yourself," he said, "You must open your inner eye. And this eye will not open unless you close the outer eyes. All sensations from outside yourself must be eliminated. Draw everything inward."

I somehow felt as though I were folding in upon myself when I meditated. At times it was almost frightening. What if some inner force just sucked everything in on itself? What would I become then—just a tiny heap of useless flesh or ash? One night when we were alone, I told the others about this.

"I've felt that, too," said Jael. "But I kept thinking it was just a problem I was having—not doing something correctly."

Martina shook her head. "It scares me, too. It reminds me of how Stephen was reduced to nothing but a heap of ashes. Perhaps the Council was right, and we are nothing but dust."

I was frightened by the blank, glassy look in her eyes. Just then Feier jumped into her lap. "Oh!" she said in surprise. "He hardly ever jumps on me."

'What does Gur-Bu'tah say?' he said.

"I heard him!" Martina cried. "Did you, too?"

We both nodded. She tentatively stroked Feier's mottled brown fur. "Why can I hear you now, and not before?" she asked him.

'I don't know,' he said. 'Perhaps your mind is more open now.'

"Maybe the meditation is helping," she sighed. "Gur-Bu'tah says when we've truly mastered meditation, our minds will bloom outward and perceive the entire Universe, all that can't be seen by the outer eyes, our senses."

"Bloom outward by drawing inward," I mused. "That seems like a contradiction. I keep trying to do just as he says, but I can't seem to get past myself. How do you two feel when you meditate?"

"I feel peaceful, usually," said Jael. "It *is* a calming way to end the day."

Martina nodded.

"But do you feel any closer to understanding God?" I persisted.

"Gur-Bu'tah says the Universe is God," she said.

"That seems to make sense, if he made it," agreed Jael.

'Wait a moment,' Feier jumped in. 'How can he be the Universe itself and have made it too? Did he make himself? In order to create something, he has to be greater than the sum of its parts. But if he and the Universe *are* the same thing, how could he be beyond it to create it?'

"Oh, Feier, you always ask such hard questions," sighed Jael.

"He's right, though," said Martina, again hearing Feier's thoughts.

'Now that you all can hear me, tell me more of what the Master has taught.'

"You've heard it all, too," I muttered. "Why do you want us to tell it to you?"

'Perhaps it will help to sort things out,' he replied.

"Okay," I nodded. "So we have a Universe which can't exist without God, because they're one and the same."

'Can God exist without the Universe?' Feier asked.

"Gur-Bu'tah says the Universe is God's body, and he can't exist without a body," Jael answered.

"But what about Stephen?" asked Martina softly. "Does he no longer exist because his body is gone?"

"I believe he does exist somewhere," Jael said quickly. "I don't know how. Maybe he has a different kind of body now, in a different kind of place, not of this world."

"I don't want to believe he's just gone forever," Martina said, trying not to cry.

"What do you think, Feier?" I asked.

'I have no answers, either. You must search for this answer for yourselves.'

"But we *have* been searching—meditating, and look-ing within ourselves, just like they've taught us here," Jael said, anger in his voice now. "There just doesn't seem to be any answer within me."

"I just can't believe Stephen is gone." cried Martina. "Deep inside, when I look within, I feel he lives somewhere—somehow—in spirit."

'Perhaps you only *want* to believe,' said Feier calmly.

"No!" she screamed suddenly, jumping to her feet.

"She's right," Jael jumped up too. "We *must* keep searching."

"Wait!" I cried, as they started out the door. "You can't leave this planet without me to pilot, and no one has asked me if *I* want to go."

"Oh, so *you* decide. Is that it?" she snorted. "The big strong leader, still our High Chieftain."

That cut deeply, and I felt myself almost stumble.

"Please," I managed to say, "Wait. Can't we talk this over some more?"

"You promised to help us find Darien, too," she added, pointing at me, her face red in anger. "Come on, Jael! Let's go talk this over as a *family*."

She turned then and led him away.

'Then I'm not part of the family,' I said to myself. 'Will I always be an outsider to her? If only I could make her see how much she means to me.'

'That will take time,' came Feier's thoughts quietly.

"Thanks for staying with me," I said. "Do you think I'll ever get through to her? And now she's even taken Jael from me."

'Wounds take time to heal,' he said. 'You should know. You have such wounds yourself.'

"So why did you have to reopen one of their old wounds?" I said.

'You mean Stephen? I didn't bring him up.'

"I guess not. I'm sorry Feier. I know you were trying to help, but sometimes you do ask all the really hard questions."

'Someone has to.'

Then both of us lapsed into silence. Feier nestled into my lap, and I closed my eyes. I didn't even try to meditate. I decided it would be easier to just sit and rest.

The others must have come back late in the evening, after I fell asleep. When I woke with the dawn, they were sprawled on the floor nearby, all of us in the same room.

***

We didn't talk too much after that, especially about deep things like God and the Universe. The anger gradually ebbed away, but I was very careful in what I said, so as not to open any more wounds. The easiest way to do this was not to talk at all. Yet my mind was still full of questions, and restless thoughts kept rising to its surface. Feier's questions kept haunting me, especially the ones about whether a God who *was* the Universe could also be its Creator. As time went by, I kept telling myself to ask the Master, but I knew his answer would be too cryptic to understand, so I didn't bother.

Then I began to wonder if we were really finding any answers here after all. The more I tried to look within myself, the less I seemed to find. And often, what I did find—anger, envy, and the like—made me not want to look anymore—especially when my longing (and yes, I'll admit it, my lust) for Martina overtook all my thoughts. On those nights, all I could do was leave our little house and walk for hours until I was too exhausted to do anything but collapse on my sleeping mat.

Then I tried meditating again, telling myself, 'I just haven't mastered it yet. Someday I will.'

But each day my restlessness seemed to grow instead. I often wondered, 'What's the matter with me? I really want to believe the ways of Pyrrhia are right, and I'm the one who's wrong.'

I think Jael and Martina would have left sooner if only I agreed. But I just couldn't bring myself to give up yet. Hadn't Gur-Bu'tah said there was no need to search outside ourselves any longer? To leave, I'd have to reject all he'd taught me, and I wasn't ready to do that.

Yet one day, as we were on our way to the fields, something outside ourselves pushed me over the edge of my indecision.

It seemed we'd been there on Pyrrhia for a long time, but I can't tell you what it was in days, weeks, or years. Time is measured differently on each planet, as each has its own speed of revolution and rotation. Gradually our bodies melded into the time-patterns of Pyrrhia.

As we neared the fields that morning, we saw a heap of dry branches by the road. Beside it was an old man we often saw working near us in the field. Just as we came to him, he lifted a hand ever so slightly, and moaned feebly.

Martina quickly knelt beside him. "He's badly hurt!" she cried. "He must have fallen with his load. Look how his back is twisted. I think it might be broken. We must help him somehow!"

"We shouldn't try to move him ourselves," said Jael. "We'll only make it worse."

"Then we have to get some help," she replied.

"But there aren't any doctors or hospitals or anything," I began, fully realizing this strange fact for the first time.

"Don't they believe in helping people?" Martina was almost in tears now.

"I'll try to get some help," I assured her.

But just as I was about to turn, a very firm hand gripped my shoulder. "What are you doing?" came a sudden sharp voice.

We all looked up in shock to see it was Gur-Bu'tah. This was the first time we'd heard even a hint of anger in his voice.

"He needs our help," cried Jael. "Or else he will die."

"No." The voice was quieter now, but still firm and powerful. "Help is only what you prefer in your ignorance."

"But isn't it good to help someone?" I asked.

"Good is nothing," said the Master. "And evil is nothing. They don't exist, except in your mind. Whatever 'IS' is what is meant to be, for everything is God. Good is only what you prefer, and evil the opposite. Both exist in God, and so they just ARE. Therefore, you must leave him, and let WHAT-IS be what it is."

We all just stood there in numb silence, with no other choice but to follow the Master into the field. But as we turned from the old man, I don't think I've ever felt worse—or more evil—in my life.

We tried to work all morning, but instead we caught each other glancing down the road to where the old man lay. At last, we came together at a corner of the field. I noticed Feier was even there, come back from his morning hunt. He wasn't supposed to eat flesh either, but so far we'd kept his hunting a secret.

For a moment, we all stood in silence there in the field. Then without a word, we moved back down the road. When we got to the place where the old man lay, we found only a lifeless form.

I stood in silence, but inside I felt as though I was coming apart—as though I myself had killed him. Soft sobs came from Martina, where she stood beside me. I reached out my hand and held her arm gently, and she didn't even pull away.

At last, it was Jael who spoke what we all were feeling, "Why do I feel this is my fault?"

"That's the whole problem," I sighed. "If Gur-Bu'tah's 'WHAT-IS' is what is meant to be, why do we feel responsible? Why does it bother us so much?"

"I can't stand it," cried Martina suddenly. "I can't stay in a place where they just let people die."

Jael turned toward me, but he didn't have to say a word. I knew he was asking if I was ready to leave with them, since they couldn't go anywhere without my ability to cross the GAP.

"Feier," I said softly, "You haven't said anything."

'You must decide, Jon. I can't do it for you.'

My mind was still a whirl of confusion. How could Gur-Bu'tah be right, if we all felt so terrible inside? Was this really only a matter of what we preferred, or was there truly a right and wrong? Our restlessness hadn't been eased here—just the opposite occurred. Wasn't that evidence enough we should continue our search, after all?

"I can't say I know for sure what to do," I muttered, "But I think any action is better than none at this point. I can't be passive the way the Master wants us to be. It doesn't feel right, somehow." I wasn't sure if I said this to all of them, or just to Feier. But then I added, more loudly:

"Come on, let's get to the ship while we've got the chance."

"Right now? We're really leaving?" they said almost as one.

"Isn't that what you wanted?"

"Yes," Jael nodded.

"Well, come on then!"

I was a few steps ahead of them all the way across the yellow plain, and through the dense herb forest. Suddenly I felt a terrible sense of urgency, as though someone was going to grab me from behind to stop me. Now that I'd made my decision at last, I knew I shouldn't look back for anything. I didn't even take us back to the city. We just headed across the hot, searing plain toward the distant patch of shimmering forest. All the way, I felt an over-powering urge to glance back over my shoulder to see if anyone was pursuing us. But I forced myself to keep looking ahead.

Then, just as we were within sight of the ship, there was the Master right in front of us, just as though he knew all along we'd come there. My heart sank. I was sure he would force us to stay.

"You have no need to leave," his voice said quietly.

"We must find Darien, our brother," said Jael suddenly.

"Yes," I nodded. Maybe he'd at least accept this reason.

"You have no need," he repeated. "You don't need your brother, or even each other. All each one needs is within himself."

"No!" I cried, and it was as though a light flashed on in my mind. "I *do* need more than my puny little self. I need my friends and their love."

"And we love our brother, too," added Martina.

"We need something beyond ourselves that we haven't found yet," Jael added forcefully.

So, there with my friends beside me, the three of us really stood together for the first time, united. And I found the courage to ask him the questions I hadn't dared to ask before, "How can your 'God' be Lord of the Universe when he is the Universe itself? How can he create himself? How can he be lord of himself?"

"Are you not lord of yourself?" he asked.

"No, I'm not." More lights seemed to flash in my mind. "I don't always do what's right. Sometimes it seems I do wrong things, even though I know they're wrong."

"There is no right or wrong," his voice continued, almost in a monotone. "Only what you prefer."

"But if 'right' is only what I prefer, why do I do 'wrong'—which I supposedly do *not* prefer?"

"Yes," Jael cut in. "And then why do I feel so badly about it afterwards? Why do I seem to have an inner sense of right and wrong?"

We could tell our words had no effect on him, but they certainly were affecting me. For now, I knew we were right in leaving. Our answers weren't here. His face still showed no emotion, but I expected him to keep trying to persuade us to stay, or even take us back by force. So, his next words were a great surprise.

"I cannot stop you. You may leave if you wish. But be warned—you won't find any answers out there."

Then, before we could say another word, he turned and walked back among the green herb stems, disappearing suddenly from sight.

"What if he's right?" murmured Martina. "What if leaving here *is* futile?"

"So what if it is?" I said. "Staying here would be futile, too. We need to continue searching, as long as we feel this need. Our restlessness is telling us something. We won't lose this feeling until we find truth. And if we don't, or it isn't out there to be found, at least we'll have tried—and not just sat here waiting to die."

At this, Jael took my hand and his sister's, turning us toward the ship. "Remember how you told me when we left Terres-City not to look back?" he said. "That's what we must do now."

"Yes, you're right."

"We must find Darien. That's what matters most to me," Martina added.

I realized this was the one hope she could hold on to for now.

So, we climbed into the ship, keeping our minds from looking back, blocking the Master's last words from our thoughts. Soon I had us hurtling across a GAP, toward the edge of that sector. Then suddenly the ship gave a great shudder, and I knew instantly something was wrong.

"What was that?" cried Martina.

"I'm not sure, something in the propulsion system, I think."

The ship continued to shudder and shake, until I removed my hands from the control panel. "I don't think we can make it across another GAP," I muttered.

"Then perhaps the Master was right," she moaned. "It was futile for us to leave."

"No, Martina," cried Jael. "We mustn't look back."

'There must be someplace out here we can land,' Feier said then. I was thankful for his changing the subject.

I looked intently at the viewer, as a tiny chunk of planet emerged into sight. "There's something," I said. "I guess it will have to do."

I tried to sound hopeful as I eased us into landing mode. At least the ship seemed responsive to simple subspace movement.

"We have to keep hoping," I whispered, looking at Feier.

CHAPTER 10

JOHAN AND THE BOOK

We ended up on a tiny planet, almost an asteroid, really. Luckily there was enough thin atmosphere to support us, if we didn't over-exert ourselves. Too often at first, I'd work too hard on the ship or climb too fast up the rocky cliffs, searching desperately for something edible. Then the dizziness would come that I'd felt in high mountains of Terres. And soon after, the retching sickness when I lost what little food was in my stomach, and I was left even weaker than before.

If I was to keep any strength or gain any nourishment from our small supply of food, I must take it more slowly and rest often in the scant atmosphere. And yet, it was this short supply of food which pressed me on, for if we ran out of food before I found a way to repair the ship, we'd starve on this forsaken bit of rock.

I felt terrible inside, but it was much more than the sickness. My whole being seemed to be crying out in pangs of regret. I was responsible for this. If only I'd listened to

Gur-Bu'tah. But it was too late to look back. Not that I was concerned for myself alone, but rather the others. It was so painful for me to watch them groping about weakly, and to think I might have brought them to their deaths here in the middle of nowhere. I think this is where I learned a heart-ache was more than just a figure of speech. For me it became a literal pain.

I'm not sure how long we were there when I reached the end of my rope. There seemed to be no time on this planet, no day or night. The star serving as it's sun was so distant that we hung in constant dawn. I'd find myself constantly looking up, hoping to see some brightening in what was the blue-black of a pre-dawn sky. But none ever came, just the same silvery starlight.

One day I was trying to see some intricate ship part in the dim light, when suddenly I threw my tool down with a cry of dismay and sat in the rock dust with my head in my hands. Soon I could feel tears wetting my cheeks and turning icy in the cold thin air. All I felt was black despair. There seemed to be no grain of hope left in me.

A small hand worked its way into mine, and I knew it was Jael's. For a long time, there was nothing but silence, as I tried to draw some comfort from his touch. Then the hand drew back and Jael threw his small arms around me.

"You mustn't blame yourself, Jon," he whispered. "Remember what you told me on that Terres ridge. Never give up."

I shook my head, wondering how he could sense my thoughts so well.

"It *is* my fault, though. If only I'd listened to the Master."

"Don't say that," he said quickly. "You know none of us could stay on Pyrrhia any longer. We found no answers there. We *had* to keep going."

"But I wonder if we'll *ever* find any answers. Maybe there just aren't any."

"There are, Jon. I don't know how I know, but deep inside I do. We mustn't give up hope. And we can't passively sit back and accept 'What-is' like Gur-Bu'tah said to."

"You mean the way he said to believe there's no good or evil, just 'What-is?' And if we saw things as the Lord of the Universe does, then we'd understand."

"That might be true," he sighed.

"One thing I know—right and wrong, good and evil, are real," I protested. "If they're only a matter of opinion, why does my heart keep telling me there is a difference between them? Why does something deep inside me keep saying there's a way things 'Ought-to-be' and *this* is not 'What-is'?"

He moved back slightly then, putting his head on my shoulder. I wasn't sure who was trying to comfort who. But gradually, the roaring in my mind subsided, and then I heard Feier.

'I feel it, too, Jon. Deep inside us there does seem to

be a sense of what is right, or what 'Ought-to-be'. And this has caused all of us to keep on searching. Perhaps we're all wrong, as Gur-Bu'tah would say, and are too far from his god to understand. But my heart won't let me think so. I think this feeling we have deep inside is God's way of calling to us, not our way of misunderstanding him.'

As his words sank in, I knew they agreed with my own inner feelings. "I hope it means something that we both feel the same about this," I sighed.

'Perhaps we'll learn more in this place, and that's why we're here.'

"Feier is right, as usual," Jael said then.

"Well, I guess we'll see more clearly when we die—if there is a place the spirit goes after death."

I let my words taper off into silence, and just sat staring at the dimly-lit landscape of rocks before us, and still I kept waiting for a sunrise which never came. I wondered if death would give any relief from this gray monotone, or if it would be more of this shadowless sameness, going on forever—no good, no evil, and only 'What-is.'

My heart felt very heavy. I reached my arm around Jael's shoulders, as we kept on staring at the bleak scene around us. Deep inside, I was wishing I could be sitting like this with Martina.

Suddenly her voice rang out, "Someone's coming!"

Jael jumped up too fast, and I had to catch him as the dizziness hit him. Martina was high above us on the ridge at our watch-post, waving her arms excitedly. Then she turned away from us and waved in the direction of a great plain I'd seen from up there.

Someone was coming? Someone else on this bit of forsaken rock? It seemed inconceivable. And yet my heart was reaching upward from its darkness, grasping for hope.

Now Martina was picking her way down from the ridge at the far end, near a narrow canyon which went through to the plain. We met her at the mouth of that canyon.

"Who is it?" Jael asked excitedly.

"How should I know!" she laughed. "He looked very small and old out there on the plain. But he saw me, I'm sure of it. He nodded and pointed toward this canyon. It was almost as though he was looking for us and expected to find us here."

Her voice was high-pitched in her excitement, and I found myself captivated by the sparkle in her eyes, though she didn't even notice my gaze on her.

"Oh, you're imagining all sorts of things," Jael was saying. "How could you tell all that from so high up?"

"I don't know," she snapped back. "I just felt it somehow, that's all."

"Stop now, you two." At my words, they both drew back, looking sheepish. "Well, should we follow the canyon to meet him?" I asked.

She nodded, and we began to pick our way through the narrow rocky crack in the ridge.

The figure was almost to the canyon mouth when we reached it. He seemed a very old man, and small, just as Martina had said. His hair was fluffy and white, and his beard flowed to his waist. The hands, appearing from the long sleeves of his brown robe, were wrinkled and delicately long as they clutched a stick for support, a stick as old and gnarled as he was. My heart began to ache again, wondering if this old relic could be of any help to us, after all.

But then reassurance came, as he stopped before us and raised his hand in greeting. I think it was his eyes that did it. There was a light in them, a fire revealing strong life within.

"We greet you, sir," I said, breaking the silence, realizing everyone was waiting for me to be the spokesman.

There was a hint of a smile above his beard.

"We seek your help if you can give it," I added.

Again the hinted smile, and this time a voice, surprisingly strong from that small frame, "Yes, I know."

Then he waited, seeming to expect me to speak again. I could think of nothing to say, so I gave our names:

"I'm Jon, formerly of Terres."

He nodded, so I continued.

"And this is my friend Jael, whom I call 'Little Brother.' And Martina, his sister."

"But she is not your sister?" he asked, and I could hear a smile in his voice now.

"We aren't related by blood," I said, wondering why his questions made me blush.

"Very well," he said in a change of tone. "I'll brush up on my Terresian. I've been in the ancient languages too long. Now, I am Johan."

"The one who shows the way!" I exclaimed, the words spilling out of my mouth before I could stop them.

His eyebrows lifted in what seemed to be surprise. "How do you know?"

"Well, someone told me its meaning once, and tried to call me that name. But I can't show the way if I don't know it. So I'm only Jon now."

"Perhaps someday you *will* know the way," he said softly.

"I hope so," I said, looking at my feet. I began to feel as though I should bow to him. "What should we call you, Lord?" I asked.

The others drew closer together as I talked to him. Looking at them now, I could see Jael's eyes going from the old man to me, full of wonder.

"No, don't call *me* Lord," Johan said. "That's only fitting for the True Lord of the Universe. I'm only human like yourself, and I live here alone, for this is where he wants me now."

These words startled me. Who was this 'he'? Did

this old man know the Lord of the Universe personally? For some reason, I was afraid to ask. Then he seemed to change the subject.

"Come. I believe you need assistance with a ship. You must show me."

As we walked to the ship, he seemed to be leading us rather than us leading him. I reflected it was as though there was a younger, livelier man hidden inside that old man's frame. Perhaps this was what showed in his eyes.

He spent a great deal of time examining the ship, commenting now and then on some detail of its construction. I could tell he had some knowledge of space ships from somewhere in his past—a great deal, in fact. I kept wondering, 'What is he doing here on this forsaken bit of rock?'

Feier heard my thoughts and joined the conversation then. 'Perhaps he's a hermit, or in exile,' he said in my mind.

Then Johan settled into dismantling the propulsion unit, completing easily the job which was so difficult for me. I could tell by the deft movements of his hands that they'd done more in their time than serve the simple needs of a hermit or exile. When we first saw him, I'd fully expected another mystic like Gur-Bu'tah. But this was no mystic who would just sit and meditate on our situation. He was doing something.

As he worked, I stayed close at his elbow, watching

those skilled hands and asking many questions in order to learn more about the intricate workings of the ship. He wasn't at all distracted by my questioning. In fact, he seemed pleased by my interest and answered each question carefully. As he finished cleaning a part of the unit, he said, "I'm glad to see you take your job seriously, Jon."

"My job?" I asked.

"Yes, your role of leadership for this little group," he nodded toward the others, who were busily polishing some bearing parts he gave them to clean. Feier was sitting alertly at Jael's feet, seeming to listen to us.

"I can tell you're a true star-voyager, Jon," he continued. "Wherever you go, you'll feel most at home with your ship, crossing the GAPs among the stars."

"How did you know?"

"I can tell by your eyes. You're eager to learn. And it takes one to know one."

I was dumbfounded. Here was a stranger saying words to me that I'd longed to hear most of my life, someone who saw in me all I'd tried to make the Star Corps see for so long. Yet now, why wasn't I sure I could believe him? As I looked up in confusion, I saw a deep knowing smile in his eyes.

"You knew your destiny all the time, but they didn't," he said softly. "And they drove you out."

"They kicked me out, so I ran away."

"You left because of their iron-clad system which left

no room for talent like yours. They could never answer your many questions."

A change in the tone of his voice made me look up. His eyes met mine, and behind the warm glow in them I saw a deep pain.

"I guess they did drive me out," I nodded.

"Yes, we're both exiles," he whispered.

"Sir, is that why you came here?"

His eyes gazed into mine, but he gave no answer. My mind was full of questions that I didn't know if I should ask. Had he really been a Star Corpsman? Was he here in hiding, or as someone's prisoner? What did he mean by saying we were both exiles? When at last he did speak, it was as though he'd read all these thoughts.

"Whether I'm here of my own will, or by someone else's, no longer matters," he whispered. "I'm where the Lord wants me. I do his will."

"What Lord, sir?" I asked.

But just then, Jael and Martina came up and handed him the finished parts. Without a word, he slipped them back into their places, as we all watched expectantly. Then he turned to us, but to my disappointment he seemed to have forgotten my question.

"Now I've done what I can," he said. "But your propulsion crystals are weak. I repaired the damage caused by using them in such a state, but it will only happen again if they aren't replaced."

"But how can we get more crystals?" asked Jael.

Martina jabbed him gently with her elbow. "Shh, let him finish!"

Johan was smiling. "You'll learn, little one," he said, looking intently at Jael. Then he turned to me. "The Lord has led you here. For on this forsaken bit of rock, the Star Corps had a cache of crystals back in the times when the Galactic Wars were in this sector. There are a few viable ones left."

"The Galactic Wars!" It was Martina who interrupted this time. "Are they near here?"

"There's no need to fear. They've long since moved the campaigns to farther sectors."

Martina's lips were beginning to quiver, so I spoke for her. "It's not that, sir. We're looking for their older brother. He's an Inland Raider."

"I see. Well, you'll keep seeking then."

"Are there star charts at this cache, too?" I asked. "We need a more complete one."

"Perhaps there are. I'll show you where this cache is, but first we must get some food for you. Come along, and I'll take you to the oasis of this rock."

Slowly, leaning on his gnarled stick, he began walking back to the canyon. We followed, trying not to go too fast for him. It seemed his work on the ship had tired him more than he let on earlier. After emerging from the canyon, we walked on the plain for what seemed ages, though there was no way to really measure the time.

Soon we were walking parallel to the ridge, moving toward the far end, where it tapered into the plain. I began to wonder if I should suggest crossing the GAP to save Johan this long walk, but had a feeling he would've suggested it, if he wanted to. Something told me Johan had his own reasons for taking us on this walk across the dim bleak plain.

At last his step began to veer toward the ridge again, near a spot where it rose high one last time before sinking into the flats. As we neared it, I thought I saw rough-hewn steps, and soon we were climbing them to a narrow passage.

At what looked like the top of the ridge, he paused, and leaning on his staff, looked down ahead of us. Following his gaze, I expected to see the other side of the ridge, and the valley our ship was in, but a strange sight greeted me instead.

The ridge seemed to split here, so that another ridge identical to the one we stood on was only a short distance from us, running parallel to ours. But below us, nestled like an island between these halves of the ridge, was a tiny valley. There was green down there and a vague sense of moisture in the air.

As we began climbing down, I realized we were on

carefully polished stone steps, very unlike the rough-hewn ones on the outside of the ridge. To one who didn't know of it, this valley was completely hidden.

Soon the steps merged into a gently sloping path as we approached the valley floor. By this time, we were surrounded by lush green vegetation, and the sounds of trickling water caressed our ears. Already, weariness was falling off me like a cast-off garment.

"This is amazing, isn't it?" Martina whispered to me. "As though some wizard created it for his own secret place."

I found I could only nod.

Ahead of us, Jael was looking around him excitedly, and Feier was darting back and forth, up and down the pathway, sniffing everything in sight. We all seemed to be revived.

Then we stepped out of the green canopy into a grassy glade. Here the light seemed somehow brighter than the pre-dawn grayness of the rest of the planet. Toward one end of this open glade was a clear blue pool with fine sand banks around it. Trees laden with some kind of fruit stood nearby, and an opening in the rock revealed a cave.

"Welcome to my humble abode, to Maiar," said Johan softly.

"It's wonderful!" exclaimed Jael.

Martina and I found ourselves speechless.

Soon we were seated by the pool, and having washed our dusty hands and faces, began to eat the fruits Johan brought. They were delicious—some tart and others sweet, and one even had a hint of the meaty taste I knew well from berry-leather. Then we all found ourselves yawning, and it felt quite natural to stretch out and nap right there on the grass.

***

I woke slowly and deliciously, as one does on a morning when there's no work to do, and no reason to get up yet. I hadn't felt this relaxed in a long time. So I lay there, letting the coolness of sleep wash back and forth across my mind. Then I began to hear words:

"Yes, my son, I can see your desire in your eyes, as well as the confusion of your heart. But you have the stronger sense of what is true and right, Jael. You must speak what you feel and help the others, even though you are so much younger."

"Feier helps me, too," Jael's voice said.

A gentle laugh came then. "Yes, you must listen to Feier when he speaks to you."

"I remember how he helped me in the Camp of the Redlarks."

I was listening to each word carefully now, my interest captured. But I lay quiet with my eyes still closed, so as not to disturb them.

"Johan?"

"Yes, child?"

"What about Gur-Bu'tah?"

"Ah, so you've been to Pyrrhia and met my friend who calls himself the Master?"

"He's your friend?" came Jael's surprised voice.

I found myself opening my eyes in spite of myself, almost echoing Jael's words. Sheepishly, I realized I was sitting bolt-upright, gazing into Johan's laughing eyes. I could tell he knew I'd been listening all along.

"Join us, Jon," he said with a chuckle in his voice. "This is important to you as well, I can see."

When I'd arranged myself cross-legged on the grass, he continued, "I call Gur-Bu'tah my friend, not because we agree, but because I pray for his soul. Long ago, in another time when we first met, we did agree and both served the Lord of the Universe. But our paths parted, and now my friend has strayed onto paths of his own making."

We both must have looked puzzled, for he chuckled again, "Such strong meat for babes! Well, I'll give you the softest food I can. Perhaps all you'll be able to digest now is the milk. First, tell me, Jael, what does Gur-Bu'tah believe, as you see it?"

For a moment, I was confused as to why he'd asked Jael to explain instead of me. But then I decided it must have something to do with the meat and the milk.

"Well," Jael began, "He said there was no use searching for answers outside ourselves. We must look within by meditating."

"And what did you find?"

"I felt as though I was folding in on myself. It seemed none of us found any answers, so we left there to continue searching and ended up here."

"Perhaps not by chance, Jael," Johan whispered, seemingly to himself. Then he looked up suddenly, "And what else did he teach you?"

"He said there was no such thing as good or evil, that everything just 'Is'. And if we could see things the way the Lord of the Universe does, we'd understand and realize good and evil are just labels we choose to put on things—good is what we like, evil is what we don't like."

"That sounds simple enough, doesn't it?"

"Oh, yes, sir. It sounded simple. But we just didn't feel right about it. Although the words made sense, our hearts and minds kept telling us otherwise. Something inside me keeps saying there really is a good and right way for things to be, and this isn't always what things 'are'."

"Can you give an example?" he asked.

Jael shook his head at this. I knew he was thinking of the old man by the road but wasn't ready to tell Johan about it.

"Sir," I said softly, "I think I have an example."

"Go on, Jon."

"If good is what we prefer, and evil is what we don't, I think life would be much simpler than it is. We'd do what we prefer, and it would be good. But something inside me gets all mixed up. When I lived in Terres-City, I spent my nights in the red darkness of the Underground, doing whatever I felt with the women and pleasures there. It was what I wanted. But even though I enjoyed these things while I did them, I had a vague feeling they were wrong. Otherwise why would I have to hide in the Underground? If right and wrong are only my opinion, why do I have this deep inner sense about them?"

"That's a very good example, Jon," Johan nodded.

I nodded to him, wishing he'd tell me more and answer my earlier question about his Lord. But I was afraid to ask him outright, so I said, "I wish life could be simpler."

"I'm afraid I can't give you easy answers," he replied.

"But why do I have this inner sense?" I finally asked. "Life would be a lot easier, I think, if I could just do as I pleased."

He nodded. "That's a very important point, Jon. You can't completely drown out this inner voice, can you— even when you want to? Perhaps this means it comes from beyond yourself. Otherwise you could control it. Some in ancient times have called it the 'conscience'."

"You know, maybe that's what I meant when I told Gur-Bu'tah I couldn't be lord of myself," I said.

Johan merely nodded, but I detected a small smile in his beard.

Out of the corner of my eye, I saw Martina had raised herself up on one elbow and was also listening intently, stroking Feier as he lay curled up beside her.

"Now let me tell you something more about the beliefs of the Pyrrhians, as I see them," Johan was saying. "They believe God—or the Lord of the Universe, if you will—is in everything. All the matter and processes around us are him. Are you understanding so far?"

"Yes, he told us that," nodded Jael.

"Good," said Johan. "And did he also tell you that the Universe is God's body, and he can't exist without it? If the Universe ceased to exist, so would God."

We all nodded at this.

"So, if everything is part of God, then both the good and evil around us are actually parts of God himself. Now do you see why the Pyrrhians *must* say there is no good or evil?"

"Yes!" I said excitedly, a light coming on in my mind. "Because if everything is God, then he has both good and evil in him. The only alternative is to say that good and evil are our own invention, and God is neither."

"That sums it up very well, Jon," he said. Then he continued, "But there's another problem, too, as we compare these ideas to the way things are—Gur-Bu'tah's precious 'What-is'. Can you see it?"

He let us sit in silence for a long while as we pondered. It was Martina who finally spoke, "I've always had a question, if this might help. If God is the Universe, and the

Universe is God, then how did everything get started?"

"Yes," Johan nodded. "So what possible answers do we have?"

"Gur-Bu'tah said everything has always been," she replied.

"That's one explanation—no beginning at all," he said.

"But the physical Universe doesn't reflect that," I jumped in. "Natural forces throughout the Universe indicate a beginning somewhere back in time."

"Yes, Jon," the old man nodded. "So *facts,* 'what-is,' seem to disagree with this explanation, yes?"

I was beginning to get excited now. To me, this was much more than a philosophical discussion.

"What other explanation might there be, then?" Johan asked.

"Well, the System theories we learned in school say everything started by chance somehow," I said. "We were taught everything began with an initial event called the Big Bang. There was nothing, and suddenly everything somehow started in a great explosion. I wonder if God started then, too."

"But Jon," he smiled, "What caused this Big Bang? What could bring all this something out of nothing?"

I blinked at him. No one had ever explained to me how this could have happened. Perhaps no one could. I wanted to say, 'Perhaps God started it.' But if he hadn't existed before the Universe, then he couldn't have done it. When the old man spoke again, it seemed he'd been reading my thoughts.

"If God didn't exist before the Universe, then he couldn't have caused the Big Bang, could he? So you were taught that 'nothing' somehow by chance caused a Big Bang that produced all the matter of the Universe out of 'nothing'."

"That doesn't make sense," moaned Jael, "Not when you really look at it. How could *nothing* do *something?*"

"It sort of short circuits my mind," said Martina.

"Indeed," Johan nodded, and I heard him chuckle again. "But there's another explanation which our poor friend Gur-Bu'tah cannot consider. And that is…"

"That God existed first!" Jael blurted out.

"Yes!" I added. "And then we can say *he* caused the Big Bang that started everything."

Johan was laughing in his beard now. "You all reason very well. Yes, you *will* find what you seek, as long as you keep the questing intelligence you have now."

He leaned back for a moment and rubbed his hands together. "So let's sum up," he smiled. "God is the source of the Universe. He started it, if our explanation is correct. And the Universe is not *him*—it's *his*. God is more powerful than the Universe and beyond it, because he created it."

"That also means we don't have to explain away good and evil the way Gur-Bu'tah does," I said quickly.

"And that's wonderful," sighed Martina. I knew she was thinking again of the old man beside the road.

Johan rose while we spoke and moved toward the mouth of his cave. "Let me show you something now," he said, rummaging through some things just inside the entrance. "Ah, here it is!" He emerged with a very ancient-looking book in a frayed black binding. He seated himself carefully again before he spoke:

"This is a very old book, my children. In fact, it's so old few know where it came from. But in parts of the Galaxy you'll still see it. It's a very unusual book, for many who read it claim that it's the words of God himself. And it has no title or author, but is simply called 'The Book'."

"The Book!" cried Jael and Martina together.

"I've always wanted to see one again," Jael continued. "Remember, Martina, how Stephen used to read it to us?"

Johan was smiling broadly now. "Ah, you do know it, then. That's very good. I won't have to urge you to read it, for I know you will." He handed the old book carefully to Jael. "Here, read the first four words to me."

Jael opened the book and turned the pages gingerly. There was awe in his voice as he read, "In the beginning God…"

"Now what is that saying to you?" Johan asked.

Jael looked up, puzzled for a moment.

"What does 'the beginning' mean?" the old man prompted.

"I guess that's the start of everything, like the Big Bang," said Jael.

Then it hit me. "It says 'in the beginning God'. That means at the beginning, God already existed. So *he did* start everything, according to The Book."

"Here's what it goes on to say," Jael read. "In the beginning God created the heavens and the earth."

"Now, what do you think?" smiled Johan.

"Well, The Book agrees with what we just figured out in our minds," I said. "And we did our best to objectively explain things as they are."

He smiled again. "As you read more, it will agree with many other things, as you discover how they *really* are." He patted Jael on the shoulder. "You keep The Book," he said. "And read it as you travel. There are many things you must learn, and many places you must go before you'll understand all it says. Some have spent a lifetime and never fathomed it all. But keep reading it, and asking questions such as I've asked you, and as you talk together, keep your senses open as well as your minds. But be sure to look at things as they *really* are before you try to explain them.

"Beware of those who explain something in a way that sounds good to them, and then keep that theory close to their heart, only because they like their explanation, not because it's true to the way things really are."

"Like Gur-Bu'tah," murmured Martina.

Jael and I nodded.

"And one other thing before I show you the crystal cache. It will help if you go to the planet Maia, if you can find it."

"Maia?" That name was familiar to me.

"Maia is the third planet revolving around a yellow star in the Centauri Sector. It's said to be humankind's mother planet."

Something connected in my head then. "My mother's name was Maia." I said.

"Yes, the word means 'Mother', which would indicate some truth in the tales that it's our original home. Perhaps it had another name in ancient times. No one knows for sure. In most of the Galaxy, Maia is ignored now. The System doesn't want us to connect with our past, so it can better control us now. Someone in ancient times said: 'A people with no heritage are easily persuaded.' And I find that to be all too true."

"But why should we go there?" asked Jael, still paging carefully through The Book.

"If it *is* our Mother Planet, as I believe it is, then the events of The Book took place there."

"Does this planet have anything to do with the name you call this place, Maiar?" Martina asked.

"I gave that name in commemoration, since it derives from 'Maia'," the old man smiled. "I'm alone now, and this place is the comfort and security of a mother's arms." He moved his hand in a wide sweep, indicating the arms of the double ridge above us.

"We feel that, too," she said, her voice contemplative now. "Of all the places we've been, this one feels the most comforting and secure. I wish we could stay."

"Everyone needs the soothing and crooning of a mother sometimes," nodded Johan, "Even when he is old."

As his words faded from my thoughts. I thought of my mother, and an old ache returned. I missed her more than I ever guessed I would. Hearing a deep sigh from Martina, I glanced up to see tears in her eyes. I knew from Jael of their mother's fate. Reaching over, I took Jael's hand. I would have taken Martina's, too, but I wasn't sure how she'd react.

"I can see great pain in your hearts," Johan's voice came then. "A pain that needs more comfort than Maiar or I can offer. Yet perhaps it will help if you express it. What is your pain?"

There was a long silence as each of us tried to decide whether we could speak of such things. The danger of opening old wounds was too great, I felt. Then Johan spoke again, "Perhaps you can just share the deep desires of your heart. That will reflect what you can't yet speak of directly."

The silence settled again until Jael finally spoke in his small wavering voice, "I'm seeking the truth, sir. Somehow, I know there's a greater truth in the Universe that's beyond human reason. But I haven't found it yet."

Johan nodded at Jael and his eyes flashed in a smile,

but he didn't speak. Then he turned toward me.

Following Jael's lead, I began,"I want to find peace. I've always been so restless, rebelling and running from one place to another, searching for something better. And I don't quite seem to find it. Some have called me Jonah, the one who runs from God'."

"Instead of Johan, the one who shows the way'," he smiled.

Then his gaze turned to Martina.

Tears were glistening in her eyes, and as she spoke it was hard for me not to reach for her hand, "What I need is hope," she began. "I just feel so—I can't find the right word—so soiled and smudged with my mistakes. I can't seem to forget them. They haunt me and keep hurting me and others."

Did she glance up at me almost apologetically? Or was I only imagining it?

"And it seems that every day I do something else wrong," she continued. "I get angry or impatient. I need hope I can become a better person, that I can truly leave my past behind."

Silence settled around us then that none of us cared to break. Once we'd expressed these deep needs, there was nothing left to say. I wasn't sure whether anything had really changed, but perhaps. I kept thinking of how Martina looked up at me. Was there a slight crack forming in the wall between us?

After what seemed a very long time, Johan spoke again, "Now perhaps each of you can see yourselves, and each other, more clearly."

I realized with a start he was echoing my own thoughts.

"I believe I do have some hope—and peace and truth—for you," his voice went on. "There's a legend, though some call it just a myth, about Maia. Often, I've found that a myth which pervades the Galaxy, as this one does, is based in facts long ago lost. It's good you've caused me to remember-"

His voice tapered off, and his eyes got a strange faraway look in them. I was afraid he might go into a trance or something, but then he looked up and smiled the most blissful peaceful smile I've ever seen.

"I know deep within your answers are there. You'll find this story to be the theme of the entire Book—that the Lord of the Universe himself became a human, on the planet Maia, long ago. It's said, because of this great sacrifice he made, that there's now a fountain which can cleanse the whole person, body, spirit and mind, of all their wrongs and mistakes."

"All of us?" said Jael.

"With no need to separate the body from the mind as we were taught?" Martina added. "And we'll be completely clean?"

"That means the answers aren't within our puny little selves, but outside us," I cried suddenly.

"From the Lord of the Universe himself," Johan smiled.

"You know," I mused. "It seems to me almost every place we've been follows the System's way of thinking, trying to tell us we each can be our own masters."

"Gur-Bu'tah sure believed that," added Martina.

"It seems like every place was a variation of telling us to be our own god," Jael nodded.

"You're very close to the correct conclusion there," said Johan. "Some call this the original sin of humans—trying to make themselves higher than the Lord by challenging his authority."

"I have a question, sir," I said suddenly. "We've seen only a small part of our Galaxy, and it seems so vast."

"Yes, and it's only a small part of the Universe," Jael added.

I was nodding to him, now. "So why would a Lord, powerful enough to make and rule all this vastness, care about anything as puny as us?"

"Ah!" Johan smiled. "This is the great Mystery of Love."

He rose then and helped each of us up. Feier jumped onto Jael's shoulder in his familiar position. He acted as though he'd been asleep, but I had a feeling the little feier-cat heard our every thought.

"I can see you recognize the truth here," Johan said, "And that you also know your great need for it. Now you must search for this planet and this fountain. I wish I could take you there myself, but it's not my time now to cross GAPs and travel the Galaxy. Your search won't be easy, but I believe the Lord will provide you with the help you need along the way."

As he said this, I was thinking how we'd found the help we needed in this unlikely place.

Meanwhile, Johan started up the stone steps. We followed him and soon were looking down from the ridge at the dimly-lit plain. We felt as though we were going from day back into night, for after our rest and refreshment in the little green valley, that barren plain looked bleaker than ever. I wished we could stay in this place of peace, like Martina said.

We stood for a long time on the edge of the ridge, on the edge of decision ourselves. Then the old man's voice began a low chant:

> *"There is a time for everything,*
> *and a season for every activity under heaven:*
> *A time to be born, and a time to die,*
> *A time to plant, and a time to uproot,*
> *A time to weep, and a time to laugh,*
> *A time to search, and a time to give up.*
> *A time to be silent, and a time to speak,*
> *A time for war, and a time for peace."*

As his deep voice died away into the stillness of the thin air, I found myself adding softly, "A time to stay and rest, and a time to search on."

His hand rested on my shoulder, and it didn't feel old and gnarled but strong and comforting. There was no need for further words.

When he finally spoke again, he said softly, "Those words are from The Book, my children. You'll find it has words for many such moments in your lives, if you heed them."

Then he lifted his arm and pointed in the direction of the tapering end of the ridge where it lost itself entirely in the plain.

"The Star Corps cache is at the base of that last bastion of rock. It will be easy to find now. You must take only the perfect crystals, the ones without any chip or crack. Jon," he turned to me, "You may use your power to take yourselves there quickly, and then to your ship."

"My power?" He took me completely by surprise.

"Yes," he smiled. "Didn't I just say there was a time for every purpose? That includes a time to walk, and a time to cross the GAP."

I smiled back, but inside I felt my mind trying to understand something deeper than I could sense.

His voice rose in pitch then, and became more decisive, "It's time for you to go, my children. Your search is very important, and you must delay no longer. Farewell, and may the Lord be with you."

He took each of our hands and joined the three of us together. Then he nodded to me, and I closed my eyes, concentrating on that last bastion of rock.

After the long slowness of waiting, the quiet of walking and talking with him, and the peace of rest, the sudden fast pace took our breath away. Time seemed to fall apart, leaving just our little group amid the calm eye of a storm.

We found the crystals easily and a nearly complete Star Chart of our Galaxy. I took only the perfect crystals, as Johan instructed, and they proved to be exactly what we needed, no more, no less. Then before we completely realized it, we were hurtling into space again, the tiny planet disappearing from our sight.

"He was a very strange man, wasn't he?" Martina said, as we released ourselves from our lift-off positions, tentatively testing the artificial gravity again.

"It was just lucky for us he was there," I nodded, "Or we wouldn't be traveling now."

"I think it was more than luck," Jael's voice came softly from where he was releasing Feier from his lift-off chamber.

We found ourselves looking at each other and feeling very strange.

At last I shrugged, "Who knows? At least we're on our way again."

'We really learned a lot from him,' Feier's thoughts came to us.

"He did seem to be a good man," Jael said.

"I think he was a wizard," said Martina. "How else could a place like that valley have appeared on that rock? It had more atmosphere than all the rest of the planet, and water, too."

"If he was a wizard, he was a good one," Jael insisted.

"How can we be sure?" she retorted. "Yes, he said nice things and helped us. But does that mean he's really good inside?"

'It was something I could feel,' Feier said then.

"Me, too," Jael added. "I could just tell somehow."

"I could see it in his eyes," I said, hoping to avert another sibling spat. "And besides, hasn't it been said 'You don't find juicy fruit on a thorny bush.' I'm not sure where, but I've heard that saying before."

"That's what it says right here," cried Jael.

We turned and saw he'd opened The Book near the back. Looking over his shoulder, I saw the words seeming to leap right off the page, "By their fruit you will recognize them. Do people pick grapes from thorn bushes, or figs from thistles? Likewise, every good tree bears good fruit."

"So, he must have been a good man, for the things he did were good," Jael said.

"It seems that way," I nodded, thinking how different Johan was from Gur-Bu'tah.

'And your book was right there to help us, just like he said it would,' Feier added.

"This is no ordinary book," Jael said, holding it gently in his hands, his voice full of wonder.

CHAPTER 11

SEEK FIRST THE KINGDOM

["Boy, Johan sure made us think about deep things," said Ginna, in Martina's voice. "I'm not sure I understood it all."

"Me neither," said Danny, in Jael's voice.

"As we continue, I think you will," Jon said. "Just bear with us, and I believe it will come clear eventually. Are you two feeling all right?

"I think I feel mostly like myself," Danny shrugged.

"Me, too." nodded Ginna. She found herself smiling into Jon's deep violet eyes.

"Okay," he said. "We'll go on with the next stage of the journey in the GAP."]

"How are we going to find Maia?" Martina asked for what seemed the hundredth time. "Especially if it's not on any of our charts? It's like searching for a needle in the dark."

"I know," I muttered. "You don't have to tell *me* that!"

"I wonder why Johan didn't just tell us where it was," she continued.

"Maybe he didn't even know. Or maybe he just made it up, the crazy old man."

"No, Jon," Jael spoke now. "I don't think so. And I think he had a reason for just telling us to search."

"What possible reason could there be for sending us on a wild chase after a nonexistent place?"

"Maybe to help us learn what we need to know, to understand the Lord of the Universe," he replied.

"Oh, there you go again with your philosophies," I muttered.

"No, maybe Jael is right," Martina cut in. "Perhaps we aren't ready for Maia yet."

"Well, all I know now is we've got to stop somewhere soon, or we'll be reduced to eating the furniture of this place," I replied, deciding it was time to change the subject. "What sort of scenic stop would you two like this time?"

"Just as long as it's not a System planet," said Martina.

"One with lots of warm sun might be nice after Johan's dim little planet," added Jael.

"But no Gur-Bu'tah. I know. Not *too* tall an order now. I can only do so much in this quadrant."

I went back to my charts again, which is what I was doing before Martina's question about Maia. We were in a fairly populous sector of the Galaxy now, with about a dozen planets to choose from. The symbols on the chart indicated four of them were confirmed System planets. Those were out for sure. Beyond these, toward the edge of the largest solar system was a lone blue planet, which seemed the right distance from its bright white star to have a tropical climate, especially if its blue color indicated the presence of water.

"How about a tropical vacation planet?" I asked.

"Sounds nice," Martina nodded.

"Okay," said Jael.

"That was almost too easy," I chuckled as I set the coordinates.

***

"This is perfect," I murmured, almost to myself, as I lay on the shining pinkish sand beside the warm green water of one of the many oceans of Paradiso, the vacation planet. The steady rumble of the breakers rolling in and crashing over themselves was lulling me to sleep. "I sure know how to pick a stopping place, don't I?"

"Ummm--" was the only sound that came from Martina. Glancing out of the corner of my eye at Jael, I could see he was fast asleep, curled up on a woven grass mat, with Feier tucked in beside him, also sleeping peacefully.

We were just outside our own little beach hut. Every visitor to Paradiso was entitled to one, for this planet's specialty was catering to those who came for rest and relaxation. All the fruit and vegetables you could want grew on the trees, just a few yards back from the beach. There were fish a-plenty to be caught with ease. If you felt ambitious, you could dig for shellfish.

But that still left a lot of time to just lie back and soak up the blessed warm sun. The inhabitants of this planet were a quiet, happy folk who delighted in dancing by the light of a campfire on the beach. No one seemed to give a care for tomorrow. All that mattered was today.

These thoughts, and the warmth of the sun and sand, were making me think of Martina, lying there so close to me. All I wanted was to roll over and touch her, perhaps even kiss her. My body ached with the desire to draw her close.

In fact, I found myself already rolling toward her, reaching for the long, silky hair that lay across her shoulder. "Martina," I whispered, "I love you. Won't you believe me?"

But I felt her shoulders stiffening already, as they always did every time I tried to touch her.

"No Jon!" her voice came sharply. "Please."

I sat up now, feeling suddenly angry. "When *will* you be ready?"

"I don't know!"

"Will you *ever* be ready?" I spat those words out too sharply, I realized.

"You don't need me," she retorted. "All you need

is a warm body. Why don't you go and find yourself a beach-girl?"

"Maybe I will!" I cried, jumping up.

This scene had repeated itself too many times now, and I was out of patience. I was too angry as I stalked away to realize this was bad timing. All I was doing was proving her right.

In my own mind I began to make excuses for myself, 'I can't go on forever with my emotions pent up inside, can I? I have to *do* something.'

Farther down the beach I saw a small group of beach-girls sitting on mats, weaving brightly colored flowers into chains. One of them had the most beautiful golden curls. As I approached, she caught my eye and smiled.

But very late that night, when I stumbled back into our hut, warm and full of wine, I didn't have the satisfied feeling I wanted. Instead there was a vague empty spot deep inside which I could never seem to fill.

'If only I could tell Martina,' I thought to myself. 'I need *her* much more than I need any beach-girl.'

***

The longer we stayed on Paradiso, the more I began to get an empty feeling inside. I couldn't put a finger on it, but one day Jael found something in The Book which struck a chord in me.

"Listen to this," he said one morning. "Here in The Book it says, 'Don't worry about what you will eat, or what you will wear. Doesn't your Heavenly Father clothe the grass of the field, and feed the birds of the air? But seek first His kingdom and His righteousness, and all these other things will be added to you'."

"You know I've been thinking about that, too," I said. "It seems like I need more than we've found here. Sure, lying on the beach day after day is wonderful, but after awhile a deep empty spot seems to grow in me."

"Me, too," said Martina.

"I guess paradise is more than just this," I sighed.

So we set off again, still searching for Maia. No one seemed to have heard of it, and no chart we saw gave even a hint. In fact, we hadn't even found the Centauri Sector. Our travels took us to many different places, as we did our best to avoid System planets.

First there was Kantah, which was a place frosted with beautiful crystals. The homes there were carved from ice, and yet were warm and cozy. They glowed with glorious colors deep inside the ice which formed their walls and floors. But even here, no one had heard of Maia.

Next we tried Grentaha, which shone a brilliant green from space. It was thickly forested over its entire surface, and no wonder—it rained there almost all the time. Clouds never stopped dropping moisture on the lush vegetation. One variation came as night fell, when the rains came down much harder—and the nights on this planet were twice as long as any other place we'd been. When the sun finally rose in the morning, billows of steam would rise from the forest floor, making banks of fog that gave an eerie look to the landscape. It was beautiful in a very wet sort of way. But as soon as the sun finally rose. The fog turned to clouds and rain was falling again. We didn't stay there very long.

After several other dead ends, we ended up on the planet Sophian. This non-System planet was a pleasant aquamarine color from space, and the people were always calm and pleasant. It seemed a very peaceful place, but I felt some inner restlessness even here, like on Paradiso. Why was I never able to settle down and take life calmly?

We stayed on Sophian for several months and tried to achieve the calm the residents showed. But somehow it kept eluding us, especially Martina. All day, her face was a picture of peace and calm, like everyone else on this plan-et, but at night when she tried to sleep, it was a different story.

CHAPTER 12

FLIGHT FROM REASON

It was a night like most on Sophian. Martina awakened us again with a screaming nightmare. Now she was sleeping peacefully at last. Her soft even breathing revealed none of the terrified screams of only a few minutes ago. I stroked her hands gently, almost gingerly, remembering how she clung to me in her dream just before she woke. But she called me 'Stephen.' She would never have held me like that when she was awake. The wall she'd built between us was still tall and strong when she was conscious.

I sighed heavily as I rose to go. Another nightmare come and gone, and we were no closer to helping rid her of them. All three of us had them for awhile here on Sophian. Yet my dreams and Jael's gradually faded, while Martina's just got worse. If only there was something I could do for her.

The fresh coolness of the night air washed over me as I stepped onto the balcony of our lodging here. A strange-looking shadow at the railing soon took shape as Jael with his feier-cat perched on his shoulder.

"Is she better now?" he asked softly.

"Well, she's sleeping again, at least."

I could see him nod, as my eyes adjusted to the dimness. Then my gaze followed his, out into the sky full of stars.

"How many planets have we been to now, Jon?"

"I've lost count. Around a dozen, I guess."

"We were so hopeful of finding our answers after Johan gave us The Book," he said. "But no one we've met, in all the places we've been, has ever heard of the planet Maia."

"Perhaps Johan was wrong, and it *is* just a long-forgotten myth," I sighed.

"Do you really believe that, Jon, deep in your heart?" He was looking at me intently now, his eyes burning with a strange light. I found I had to look away.

"I sure wish I could help your sister," I murmured. "What I think she needs is love, and I want to give it to her, but she keeps pushing me away."

To my surprise he slipped his hand into mine. "I know, Jon," he whispered.

I squeezed his hand, trying to convey some of the affection his sister refused to receive. "If only she could let out some of those fears she has bottled inside, then maybe she'd see how much I really love her."

"She's had a hard time." he sighed.

"We all have."

"Yes, but her problem goes further back than the Redlarks. She folded inside herself when Stephen died, and shut everyone out, even me. It's as though she's determined to never lose a loved one again."

"And the only way she can do that is to never love anyone, right?"

"I'm afraid so. That even includes me. For awhile she pretended to love Jason, though."

"The same Jason I know? With the fiery red hair?"

"Yes. I first met you at his house, remember?"

"Now that you mention it. So *she* was 'Jason's Woman' I kept hearing about in the Underground."

"It was just a game she was playing, to try to hide from her own feelings. You know how the Underground is."

I was surprised to hear one as young as Jael talking about the Terres Underground as though he knew all about it. Again, I wondered how he could be so mature beyond his years. Perhaps it was partly Feier's influence.

Then I sighed, "I guess she was just playing games with the Redlarks, too, with Rigan and me."

"It's hard to say. The influence of all kinds of spirits was very strong there."

I shuddered suddenly, remembering what power those evil spirits could wield over mere humanity.

"But what can we do for her, Jon?" I was thankful his voice interrupted my thoughts.

"Your love reached her once, Jael."

"Yes, when we fled the Redlarks, and broke her trance. You said it was my love that broke through. But I don't know if there's any more I can do. Perhaps it's time for your love to reach her, Jon."

"But she'll never give me a chance. She calls out for Stephen in her sleep. I can never take his place."

"You shouldn't try to. But Jon, I think we need to leave this planet for her sake."

"Leave Sophian already? But I thought this, of all places we've been, could help her. Here they've learned inner control. The people here are good examples of that."

'Can't you see?' Feier said suddenly. 'They're just being stoic here, putting on a mask of control, burying their real feelings. That's the last thing Martina needs. She needs to open up and let all those pent-up emotions out, the good and the bad.'

"She seems to let out her share of emotion often enough in her shows of temper."

'Oh, Jon,' Feier's thoughts continued, 'Those are just small flashes at the surface, barely showing all the rest she has lying underneath.'

"Well, she does seem to be having more nightmares since we came here."

'She sure is. Because the more she tries to lock

everything inside, the more things leak out.'

"I wonder how the Sophians let things out," I mused. "Perhaps they have an Underground here, too."

"I don't want to stay to find out," said Jael quickly.

'Don't you see?' Feier asked. 'This place is only a slight variation on the same theme we've found everywhere—mankind trying to control his own spirit and body with his mind—and failing.'

"How do you know so much, Feier?" I asked.

'Jael and I together communicate many things.'

"Yes, Jon, we're sort of like two minds in one body sometimes."

'Jael has an exceptional mind to receive so much,' Feier added.

"So, Feier, are you some spirit sent to guide us?" I asked.

'No. I'm merely a telepathic animal,' Feier replied. 'Yet under Jael's care, I find my powers heightened. We have some special chemistry which makes us more than the sum of our parts. But you and Jael have something between you, too, Jon.'

I was wondering what this meant. Yes, I felt a sort of kinship with the boy. I embodied it in my name for him—Little Brother. But it seemed we hadn't tapped the full potential of this power yet, whatever it was.

"So what do you and Feier think we should do now, Jael?"

"Feier and I think you should make that decision," he shrugged.

Faced with this, I suddenly felt very tired, and sat down heavily on the floor of the porch. Jael settled beside me, and Feier jumped down from his shoulder and curled into my lap. We sat for a long time, just feeling the cool of the night air.

"So, it appears to be time to move on—*again*," I sighed. "So many places we've been, and never any real answers. Every place has a different philosophy, but when we look deeper they all have the same basic pattern, humans trying to find their own way to God, or enlightenment."

"Even non-System planets seem to have a System-mentality," Jael sighed.

"Sometimes I feel our journey is futile, that there are no answers to be found. Maybe the search is all there is, a never-ending odyssey."

"That could be true," nodded Jael.

'All the more reason to keep moving on,' Feier said.

"It is?"

'Yes, because if the search itself is all there is, then where will we be if we give it up? Nowhere.'

"Your logic astounds me," I said bitterly. "But you're right. We'll take off in the morning."

With that, the three of us curled up right there on the porch and slept out the rest of the night.

Early the next morning, we took our few belongings

and what preserved food we could get on Sophian and headed back to where I'd secured the ship. This procedure was all-too-familiar to us now. That morning, as Sophian's pinkish-toned sun began to edge above the distant hills, I wondered if this was how I would spend the rest of my life, wandering aimlessly through space.

Yet once we were back in space, my mood lifted as I felt the precise responses the ship made to my thought patterns. Yes, if this was my destiny, so be it. At least out in space I was in control, unlike our experiences on planet surfaces. Johan had been correct—I was happiest out among the stars.

After we crossed a couple of GAPs, I began to feel a strange quivering in the ship. At first it was gentle and stopped intermittently. But each time it returned, the shaking was more pronounced. My heart was already beating quickly by the time the others noticed it.

"What's wrong, Jon?" Martina asked first.

I shook my head. "Feels like the propulsion system again," I shrugged.

"But we got new crystals from Johan."

"That was many GAPs ago."

Just then the ship gave a violent lurch, cutting off my words. For a few seconds, everything whirled around me, and I completely lost all my bearings. Then I managed to steady the ship for a minute, though I could still feel it shuddering.

"Quickly!" I cried to the others. "Secure yourselves in your seats. We may have to crash land."

"What about Feier?" came Jael's small voice.

"He'll be safer in his compartment."

"But what if there's no one to let him out after?"

"All right! Hold him then. But strap yourself in securely."

I barely said these last words before the ship began to spiral again. We were falling out of the GAP back into some place and time, and I had no idea where or when. I didn't even know what sector we were in.

My mind was whirling, too, wondering what the odds were that we'd hit something. I didn't think I could last much longer in this spinning nightmare. Then the feel of the ship changed again. Could we be in some planet's gravitational field? I felt heat through my hands on the controls. We were definitely passing through atmosphere, and the friction was creating intense heat. For better or worse, our ride would soon be over.

"Hang on!" I heard my voice cry out. "We're crash landing!"

The heat grew more intense, and I felt the world going black, closing in on me. The last thing I heard was Martina's cry:

"Help! Oh, Stephen, help me!"

***

Something was getting in my face. I batted at it, but soon it was back. Must be some pesky bug. I tried to swat it again, and a sharp pain shot through my arm. I sat up, trying not to cry out, and my head began to spin. Then I felt a small furry form climbing into my lap and heard a loud mewing.

'Jon, are you all right?' came a familiar voice in my mind.

"Feier? Is that you?"

By this time, I'd managed to open my eyes. Pieces of space ship were scattered all around me. Then an acrid, smoky smell reached my nose. Fire!

"Where are the others?" I cried.

'I've found Jael,' came Feier's reply. 'Come quickly!'

He was off with a bound, and I followed as best I could. Except for a sharp pain in my shoulder, I seemed to function fairly well, though shakily.

Soon we reached the small bundle that was Jael's body, lying dangerously close to a brush fire, evidently started by our crash. Gritting my teeth against the pain in my shoulder, I lifted him as gently as I could, and moved him to a patch of lush greenery which I hoped would be less likely to burn.

"Feier, stay with him! I have to find Martina!"

Urgency gripped me. Ahead, I could see only billows of smoke. Where could she be? Yes, she'd called for Stephen! So she'd probably gone into some nightmare state before the crash. Perhaps she was still in her seat. But where was that seat now?

Then I made out a large shape through the heat haze; part of the main cabin was still intact. I squeezed through a jagged opening and saw two seats and part of the console.

Coughing from smoke and fumes, I groped my way to one seat and found her still strapped in. She'd fallen forward, hitting her head on the console. Fumbling, I managed to get her free of the harness, and put her over my good shoulder. But how to get out of here? I could never get through that jagged hole with her on my back. I groped my way along the console, and abruptly the floor was gone beneath my feet. Both of us rolled. When we stopped, I landed on top of her and she moaned. Good, at least she was still alive.

We were in a parched area, already burned by the fire. I picked her up again and stumbled toward some tree-like shapes to my right. Here the smoke seemed thinner, and I paused for a moment to catch my breath.

"Feier, where are you?" I gasped.

'To your left—behind you,' came the quick reply.

I moved as quickly as I could through the tall greenery but had to stop to rest every few steps. Fits of coughing struck me as my lungs tried to clear themselves of fumes. At last I reached him, and laid Martina's body gently next to her brother's.

"Well, what now, Feier?"

I really wasn't surprised when his only reply was to begin licking at the wound on Martina's forehead.

Her face was covered with blood. Fortunately, it all seemed to have come from a single cut just above her eyebrows. The bleeding was slowing now, under Feier's ministrations. Using a couple of strips ripped from my shirt, I made a good snug bandage. Then I turned my attention to Jael.

His breathing was very shallow. In fact, he stopped breathing altogether once or twice, and I found myself holding my breath in sympathy. But then he'd take a gasping breath, and his chest would begin to rise and fall again. I couldn't see any outward injuries, but he wasn't doing well. I managed to get my jacket off, though pain stabbed through my shoulder with each movement. Then I covered him with it, hoping that at least some warmth would help.

'You should immobilize your shoulder,' Feier said. 'It's probably dislocated.'

"I will when I have time," I snapped aloud to him.

'There's not a lot you can do for them now,' he continued calmly.

I looked over at Martina. My improvised bandage had stopped the bleeding, and Feier had cleaned her face. She seemed to be resting peacefully enough, but Jael began to toss and turn just then, moaning softly.

I held him down gently so he wouldn't hurt himself.

"Why is he having convulsions?" I heard myself ask.

'He probably has internal injuries from being thrown from the ship,' said Feier.

At last Jael quieted again. I held his hand, feeling how clammy it was.

'Oh, Little Brother," I murmured, "Please don't stop fighting to live. I need you."

Periodically, Feier came over to lick his face, cleaning the beads of clammy sweat from his brow. I never let go of his hand, but looked at Martina often, wondering if her blow on the head had done much damage.

The sky began to darken, and the fires around us dropped to a slow smolder. A chill breeze wafted my cheeks. Feier drew closer to where I sat between my two friends, wondering how long this lonely vigil would last.

I didn't leave either of them for what seemed an endless cold night. Neither stirred much, but I tried to be sure they were at least still breathing.

A crackling sound in the brush woke me. My first thought was, "Fire!" As I jerked awake, hot pain shot through my shoulder again. Then through the early morning mists, I saw a figure in some sort of green shirt and leggings. Fringes hung from the arm seams of the shirt, looking like it was made from some sort of animal skin. He made a quick motion with his head, and more figures loomed up behind him.

"Hello?" I said in common System speech.

He nodded but didn't say a word, so it was hard to tell if he understood or not.

My heart began pounding as he stepped toward me. What was he going to do? He knelt beside me and began to feel my shoulder gently. Suddenly I felt intense pain, and everything flashed red and white before my eyes.

He made a grunting sound but spoke no words I could understand. Then I felt him place my arm across my chest, binding it to my body. For an instant, I caught his gaze and he nodded, patting my arm. Was he trying to reassure me?

Next, he rose and knelt by Jael and Martina in turn. Another rustling in the brush came suddenly, and I saw his companions with some sort of carriers made from swaths of cloth and long poles. There were six of these men altogether. We were definitely at their mercy, I knew. As they began to lift Jael onto one of the carriers, I cried, "Be careful! He has internal injuries."

Probably no one understood me.

A gentle hand took my good arm just then and guided me to another carrier. As I lay back, I heard Feier mewing loudly. The man standing over me smiled and picked up the feier-cat, placing him on my chest.

From their dress, I took these people for primitive woodsmen, but their actions were very gentle and controlled.

'I wonder where they're taking us?' I thought to Feier.

'It doesn't matter, really,' he replied. 'At least we're not lying in the forest, waiting to die.'

I nodded. As usual, he was right. Then I let myself lie back, as two of them picked up the carrier, one at each end. I could sense the other two carriers moving nearby. I let go then, knowing that our fate was out of my hands.

This is the last thing I remember for a long time.

***

Had the world gone dark again? Was it night or day? My eyelids felt too heavy to lift. I could feel someone's presence, though. Then a cool, gentle hand was in mine, a woman's hand.

***

Sometime later, streaks of light began to appear, and I found my eyes trying to focus on them. Was there a shape emerging? Yes, a face! At last, I got my eyes to focus and saw Martina sitting beside me, a bandage around her forehead.

"The fever's broken." she called to someone behind her. "He's awake."

"Martina," I tried to get my mouth to work. "Are you…"

"I'm fine," she smiled, and I felt a warmth flow through

my body. "I had a concussion, but I finally convinced them I *had* to sit with you."

I began to think, by the sound of her voice, that something had changed while I was unconscious.

"But I just hurt my shoulder."

"They say you developed an infection," she said, understanding my unasked question. "It spread throughout your body. But now the fever has broken. Oh, Jon," she squeezed my hand tightly.

I wondered what else she wanted to say. Did I dare hope the wall she'd put between us was coming down?

"How's Jael?" I murmured, feeling very tired all of a sudden.

"You must rest now," she said softly, seeming to ignore my question.

I knew she heard me. What was she hiding? I wanted to jump out of the bed and find out. Perhaps Jael was dead. I had to know! But sleep was engulfing me from behind, and soon my world was swallowed up in blackness.

***

When I woke again, I felt a little stronger. A small hand was resting on my arm. I opened my eyes, wondering if I'd dreamed Martina was there. But no, there she was, dozing in a chair beside my bed. Her bandage was gone now, and only a slim scar showed above her left eyebrow.

Beyond her, I could now see another form on the bed next to mine. The face was so pale, almost like death. Yet there was some life—slow shallow breathing, through tubes inserted into his nostrils. Then with a shock, I realized the figure was Jael. I tried to get up and go to him, but Martina woke. My head began to swim with dizziness, and I fell back.

"All we can do is wait and hope," she whispered, seeing my gaze fastened on that still, small form beside us. Then to my great surprise, she planted a kiss on my cheek. "At least I'm not going to lose both of you," she murmured. She must have seen my eyes widen in surprise, for she smiled. "I tried to wall myself in, so I'd never lose anyone again, like I lost Stephen. But I failed to keep your love out, Jon. Because you refused to stop loving me, no matter how awful I was to you. And when I saw you two lying here, I knew it was too late to stop caring—I already loved you. My only choice was to let all those pent-up feelings out."

Tears were glistening in her eyes now. "Jon, can you forgive all the unkind things I've said and done? I thought I could drive you away from me, but you just kept right on caring. And when I thought I might never have this chance to ask your forgiveness—well, now I know how much I love you." Her voice broke off with a sob.

I reached a trembling hand to wipe the tears from her cheek. "It's all right."

"No, it isn't all right—what I've done. But will you forgive me?"

"Of course, I will," I whispered, drawing her into my embrace as best as I could. I'd wanted to do this for so long. "I love you, Martina," I murmured into her soft brown hair.

As the days flowed past, I gradually became stronger. Soon Martina and I were permitted to take short walks outside. This planet was very lush and green, at least in the area we were in.

Jael remained in a coma, not responding to anything as far as we could tell. My heart ached every time I looked at him. It helped so much to have Martina there beside me, holding my hand, or leaning close to me as I drew her into my arms. At least now we had each other.

One day, as we were strolling beneath some broad-leafed trees, I asked her about this place.

"This planet is called Platius," she said. "Many of them speak a little System-speech, so I've been able to communicate."

"It's not a System planet, though?"

"Not that I can tell. There doesn't seem to be a System City controlling everyone."

"Are they Rebels then?"

"They say they're not. When I asked, one man just laughed and said, 'The Rebels hide in the mountains, like mice in burrows!' These people here in this city call themselves the Nosticenes. It means 'Those of the Special Knowledge.' And they know The Book."

"They do?"

"Yes, very well, in fact."

"Do they know anything about the Fountain?" I was beginning to get hopeful now. Perhaps we might find our goal at last.

"They just shrug when I ask about the Fountain," she replied. "They tell me it has no importance anymore, that it was for another time and place. 'Now we have the Special Knowledge', they say."

"But what's this 'Special Knowledge'?"

"I haven't been able to get anyone to tell me yet."

"Why don't they tell, if it's so important to them?"

"I don't know. They seem to think it gives them prestige and power to have this secret knowledge. They treat me like a small child who couldn't possibly understand."

I could hear the anger and frustration in her voice now. I squeezed her hand to try to let her know I understood. When she smiled up at me, I thought my heart would leap right into my throat.

"I think there's another group on this planet besides the Nosticenes, though," she said then.

"Rebels?"

"Besides them, too. One day Rehoba, the doctor here, muttered something about Colassenes. When I asked who they were, he pointed east and cursed. The Nosticenes and Colassenes must be very bitter enemies."

"Are the Colassenes in a System City, then?"

"I don't think so. I asked the nurse later, and she only shook her head, 'No System on Platius.' There's something strange here, though, with all these secrets and stuff."

The next day, I decided to take things into my own hands. Perhaps they wouldn't treat me as much like a child. When the doctor came on his rounds, I was armed with questions that I hoped would get answers. And I made sure Martina was there with me, so we'd have two sets of ears to listen.

"Good morning," said Rehoba, as he walked in with his quiet, smooth gait. He almost seemed to float whenever he moved. "How is my young patient today?"

"I am feeling much better, sir," I said.

"Yes, I can tell by your voice," he smiled.

As he began examining my shoulder, I jumped right into my questions. "Sir?" I began, using my most respectful tone, "You know that our ship crashed, and we're going to be here for a long time, it seems. We like your planet very much and would like to stay, if we may."

"Indeed?"

"But we're curious about your society. Could you explain your basic beliefs to me, please?"

"Well, perhaps," he began. "We Nosticenes are the people of the Special Knowledge."

"Yes, sir. I've heard of this." I glanced at Martina. "But what is this Special Knowledge?"

"I'm afraid I couldn't explain it so you would understand," he said quickly. "It's very deep. You must be purged of your sicknesses first, and then we can deal with the inherent evil of your bodies. If you attain the Level of Separation, then perhaps you'll be ready to understand."

"Level of Separation?" I asked as calmly as possible, hoping to lead him to reveal more.

"Separation of your good nature from your evil nature, of course," he said.

"How can that be done, sir? Forces of good and evil are so intertwined within human beings."

"It's so simple that everyone else has missed it!" he exclaimed. Then he leaned closer and whispered, "It's the body which is evil. Good resides only in the spirit, the inner being."

Suddenly he drew back, apparently realizing he'd said too much. He reached for his monitor and placed it close to my chest. "Ah, yes, your heartbeat is stronger now. Very good." He placed a small monitor on my forehead for a moment. "Body temperature normal for this time of day. I would say you're quite healed, young man."

"But I don't understand something, doctor," I tried again. "If my body is evil, why have you gone to such efforts to heal me?"

"Healing is a purging of evil," he smiled. "Once the evil is purged, the Separation process can begin."

Martina moved to Jael's bedside while he examined me. Now Rehoba stepped towards the still, pale form.

"What about healing Jael?" she asked. I could hear her trying to keep her voice from wavering.

"There's great evil here," said Rehoba, almost shuddering. "We may have to resort to the Final Separation with him, and free his spirit from his body altogether."

I could see Martina flinch at this, and quickly stepped to her side, putting my arm around her waist.

"Hopefully, he'll be better tomorrow," I said as calmly as I could.

"Yes, I hope so," Rehoba shook his head. "Well, I'll see you tomorrow. Perhaps we can determine your Separation schedule then."

By the time he left, Martina was trembling noticeably. "I don't like the sound of that Final Separation," she whispered.

"Neither do I. All this separation business sounds too much like the System to me. I've got to find out more about this place. We can't make any intelligent decisions without more data. We're too secluded in this infirmary."

"That's exactly what they want, I think," she hissed. "To draw us in before we know the whole story. By the time we learn the truth, they'll have us in their power."

"Not if I can help it. By the way, where is Feier? He was with me when the men in green carried us from the forest."

Martina lifted a cover beside Jael's still form. Next to him lay Feier, also very still, and breathing very slowly.

"What's he doing?" I asked.

"I'm not sure. He seems to have gone into some kind of hibernation while Jael has been unconscious. Maybe he's sharing Jael's experience."

"Or maybe he's trying to help heal him," I mused.

"I hope it works," she sighed.

"Anyway, we can't ask *him* for any ideas right now," I shrugged.

"What *can* we do?"

"I've got to find a way to slip out of this place and do some exploring in the city outside, see if I can learn anything that might help us. And I think I'd better get on with it. We don't know how much time Jael has."

"So what *are* you going to do?" she asked again.

"I think I'd better keep my plan to myself," I said. "That way they can't punish you if I fail. You'll know nothing of it. Just stay close to Jael, and make sure they don't try to do anything with him while I'm gone."

Suddenly she pulled me close to her in a desperate embrace. "Can't I come with you, please?" she sobbed into my shoulder. "I'm so afraid!"

I stood holding her for a long time, trying to soothe away her fears as I smoothed her hair. It was killing me to leave her like this, not knowing if I would ever enjoy her long-awaited embrace again.

But I tried to be strong for both of us as I said, "Some great power has preserved us through many dangers so far. We must keep trusting that all will be well and we'll be together again very soon." I nodded toward Jael. "He needs you right now. I'll try to come back before Rehoba comes tomorrow, I promise." As I reluctantly pulled away from her embrace, I prayed I was going to be able to keep this promise. My eyes began to burn with tears. "I won't be long," I whispered.

"Now that I've finally found you, I can't lose you, Jon!" she sobbed.

"I love you," I said, kissing her quickly. "But I must go."

"I know."

Then I turned and ducked out the door, before either of us could change our minds.

CHAPTER 13

SPECIAL KNOWLEDGE

No one was in the hallway outside our door, but as I rounded the next corner, someone was coming with a tray. There was a small closet near me, so I ducked into it. In the darkness, I tried to formulate some kind of plan to get outside the infirmary.

As my eyes adjusted to the darkness around me, I could see dim shapes of clothing hanging from hooks. I reached for one and realized it was a coverall, such as the infirmary orderlies wore. Perhaps this would be just the thing.

I slipped into one, and the fit was reasonable. There was a hand-sweeper hanging on the back of the door, which I also took. This would complete the disguise, I hoped. Then I listened at the door for some time, until I was sure the hallway was empty.

Opening the door, I stepped out quickly and closed it as quietly as possible. Then I began walking casually down the hall, carrying the sweeper, as I'd seen the orderlies do.

I'd just rounded a corner when a voice snapped, "You, orderly!"

I jumped and turned. A doctor I'd never seen was walking toward me. "They need assistance on the first floor, rear door. Be quick about it!" she said.

"Yes," I nodded, and turned to look for the way to the first floor.

"Just take the tube—it's faster," she snapped, pointing to an oval door to my left.

I almost saluted, but then tried to look subservient instead.

As I stepped into the oval tube opening, I was relieved she didn't follow me. Once I was inside, a soft chime sounded. "Direction?" came a mechanical voice.

"Uh—lower level," I said.

The tube let out a pneumatic hiss as it began to drop. When it stopped, I found myself stepping into what appeared to be a basement service area. Evidently 'lower level' was not the same as 'first floor.' Perhaps this was better, though, for no one was around. Now if I could find a service entrance, and soon I did. A boxy-shaped vehicle was pulled up to a loading dock, and a few boxes were set inside it. I wasn't sure whether it was being loaded or unloaded, but I gambled on the latter, and climbed into the back of the vehicle, closing the door behind me.

In a few minutes I heard voices, "Time to call it a day, eh, Toah? Night deliveries are complete." This sounded promising.

"Right. Now for some mental relaxation."

"And breakfast."

"Ah yes, the necessary evils of supporting the body, eh?"

"You're sure into this Separation stuff, Toah. What for?"

"It means moving up in this city, my dear Koral. Doesn't that have any meaning to you?"

"Oh, I don't know. Give me a good drink and a good woman. That's all I need in life."

"You'd better take care, Koral. You're sounding like a Colassene. You could get yourself banished if the wrong ears heard you say that."

"Aw, maybe that wouldn't be so bad."

Their voices faded from my hearing as they climbed into the vehicle's cab and started the engine humming. Soon we were moving slowly, and I sighed, hoping I was going to learn more about this strange city.

When the vehicle stopped again, I held my breath, hoping they wouldn't check the back of the vehicle before they left. I stared at the door, wondering what I could do if they opened it. But the door remained closed, and soon I heard their footsteps fading into the distance. Then came a pneumatic hissing sound, followed by silence. I waited a few minutes longer, then cautiously opened the door.

No one was in sight, so I hopped out quickly and ducked into the nearest doorway, finding myself in some sort of locker room. Uniforms such as the delivery men were wearing hung on the wall opposite me, so I quickly traded my orderly uniform for one. I glanced around the room, wondering which of the end doorways led to the outside. Just then, a figure stepped through one of those openings.

He was slightly taller than me with closely cropped dark hair. I was relieved when he smiled at me. "You're new here, aren't you?" he said.

"Yes," I said, smiling back.

"I'm Kotam," he nodded.

"My name is Jakol," I said, hoping this name would sound more Nosticene than 'Jon'.

"Going off duty?" he asked.

I nodded. He sat down on one of the benches and took off his uniform. Feeling uncomfortable, I decided to sit on an adjacent bench. Then he stood and opened a locker, taking out some clothes.

"Don't you want to change into street clothes?" he asked.

"I—uh—forgot them."

"First day on the job, eh?"

"I was just nervous, I guess," I said, hoping this sounded plausible.

"No matter," he smiled. "Say, would you like to join me for some sustenance?"

"You mean breakfast?"

"Sure, if you like."

"I'd like that very much."

"Good." He was dressed now. "Come along then, Jakol was it?"

"Yes."

I followed Kotam through a series of corridors, until at last we emerged into the open air, and my first view of the city of the Nosticenes. I was struck by the barren sameness of the streets as we walked. All the buildings were low-slung rectangles of a drab gray color. There weren't any trees, though we'd seen some on the infirmary grounds, and none of the buildings had any ornamentation to break up their monotony.

After turning a few corners, Kotam stopped beside some sort of transit cube, placed his hand over a green circle, and stepped in. As soon as I stepped in beside him, the familiar pneumatic hiss started. When the motion stopped and we stepped out, I saw we were in a more central part of the city. Here the buildings were bigger, but still the same dull shapes and colors. Off in the distance I could see one shimmering shape rising high above the rest. With a start, I realized it looked much like Neptune Spire in Terres-City.

Kotam followed my gaze. "The Tower of the Spirit is beautiful in the morning sun, isn't it?"

"Yes," I nodded, "It surely is."

"Well, this is as good a place as any for breakfast," he

steered me toward a door nearby. "Not much variety here in Urbis, what with the Nosticenes being so ascetic." He leaned close to me and grinned as he whispered, "Now Colasse is a different matter, they say. Everything there a body could desire."

I nodded, smiling what I hoped looked like a knowing smile.

Once we seated ourselves at one of the white tables inside, he pressed a button at the edge, and two plates of drab-looking food appeared. "Very nourishing, they say," he nodded to me. "But not much choice. We aren't allowed to enjoy such things as eating, are we? Mustn't indulge even one bodily pleasure."

I could hear the mocking tone in his voice and wondered what all this meant. It was becoming clear that the Nosticenes were strict ascetics. But not everyone in this city—what had he called it, Urbis?—seemed to be a true Nosticene. At least not the common laborers. There appeared to be a tiered structure to society here. Kotam seemed to be open to discussing things, so I decided to go out on a limb.

"Have you been scheduled for Separation yet?" I asked him quietly.

He shrugged.

'So far, so good,' I thought to myself.

"I don't know if I will," he said. "They say I must if I expect to advance any in my work. And I have to deny my body just to live here in Urbis, anyway. But, I don't know. Say, would you like to go see the Separations today?"

"They let us watch?"

"Sure, all the time. Haven't you ever been?"

The surprise in his voice told me I'd made a big slip. "Oh, I just never had time, I guess."

"Well, do you have any other plans today?"

"No. Sure, let's go." I tried to sound excited.

"Okay, finish your stuff, so we won't be late."

When we'd eaten the nearly tasteless food, we went back to the tube terminal and re-entered. When we emerged this time, we were near the tall spire I saw earlier. What had he called it—the Tower of the Spirit? That certainly fit with my conclusions so far. The Nosticenes venerated the spirit above the body. I still had an overpowering feeling there was a lot of System influence here. This tower could be Neptune Spire, and the emphasis on denying the body and elevating the spirit was very familiar. My next question was, where was the Underground? The System always needed to provide some outlet for those bodily passions. What did the Nosticenes do? Perhaps I'd find out soon.

I followed closely behind Kotam as he entered the Tower of the Spirit, and suddenly, we left the drabness of Urbis behind. The walls around us shimmered with multi-colored light, and I blinked my eyes in wonder.

"The only beautiful place in the city," Kotam whispered in my ear. "That's because it's the place of the spirit, and only the spirit is good and beautiful."

All I could do was nod. As we wended our way through the rooms and corridors, I was amazed at the beauty all around me. Then I realized this was probably one of their most powerful tools for luring people into the Separation ceremony, to give them only one place of awe in otherwise drab lives.

Ahead of us loomed a massive door. Just as we got there, the huge door swung open to admit the crowd of spectators waiting before it. Inside was a huge auditorium with a ceiling rising so high it disappeared into the spire of the tower. The seats were arranged in a circle around a large central stage. On this stage was a black cylinder with openings around its sides and no cover above it. I sat down beside Kotam, hoping he'd continue to explain things as well as he had so far.

For a long time, we sat in silence as others filed in and seated themselves around the stage. I was thankful we were in one of the rear rows. Somehow, I didn't want to be too close to that ominous black cylinder.

"When does it start?" I finally whispered to Kotam.

"Soon," he nodded. "The Proctors are about to close the doors."

"They're shutting us in?" I felt a shot of fear.

"Don't worry," he smiled. "They just don't want anyone leaving too soon and missing the best part of the show."

I nodded, hoping he was right. There came a loud

boom as the doors closed. I had no choice now.

Soon I heard a low steady hum in the air, gradually getting louder and slightly higher in pitch. It had the strange effect of making me feel drowsy. Then came an overtone of sweet plaintive melody.

"They call this the Song of the Spirit," whispered my companion.

"Like the call of the spirit over the mundane sameness of life," I whispered back.

"Very good, Jakol." he smiled. "You learn quickly."

Something in the tone of his voice made me wonder what he really meant by this, and I turned to look at him, but he was wearing his usual smile. Just then, the lights around us went dark. The only light left was a single beam streaming down from the top of the tower. Just the center of the stage was illuminated.

Then shadowy forms moved onto the stage, standing in the edge of that light. An eerie-sounding chant in a language I couldn't understand began to rise from the figures. Each of them was robed in black, and each moved one slow step at a time toward one of the openings in the rim of the cylinder.

"They're chanting for their spirits to be freed from the confines of their bodies," Kotam whispered.

I nodded silently.

Now the chant rose to a high pitch, nearly screeching in my ears. The figures disappeared into the cylinder, and suddenly the chanting stopped. Then a new sound began, a roaring like the wind. Underneath there was a crackling sound of fire.

A red glow appeared through the openings of the cylinder. There *was* fire in there, or at least something that sounded like it, but there was no heat that I could feel. Still, flames seemed to leap out of the top of the cylinder. If it was a projection or image, it was a very convincing one.

Suddenly a sharp cry rang out through the air in the hall, and out of the top of the cylinder rose the shapes of bodies. They floated ever upward into the top of the spire, and on each face was a look of ecstasy.

"Their spirits are separated now," Kotam whispered in my ear. "There they go, rising into the Tower of the Spirit—to dwell there forever in peace."

I tried to look closely at what was happening up there, but it was too distant to see clearly. 'What's really going on here?' I wondered. A faint shimmer around the rising bodies made me think perhaps they were really holograms.

"Are their bodies destroyed?" I asked quietly.

"Not really. They'll still be living among us but will be 'Separated' and set aside for the Special Knowledge. No one but the initiated knows what it is. This is the first step to Final Separation."

"So what does this really do for them?" I couldn't help but ask.

"They say there are no bodily desires or impulses after this—no lust, hunger, and the like. They must maintain their bodies for life among the rest of us for a time yet. The goal here in Urbis is to separate from your body day by day, until the end."

By this time, the shimmering figures disappeared into the top of the tower, and slowly the red light glowing all around us faded, as the normal auditorium lights came back on. Gradually, the people rose and moved toward the huge doors, walking back through the dazzling halls and out into the drab world of Urbis.

"Well, what do you think?" Kotam asked, once we were outdoors again.

"I don't know. It reminds me of the System."

"Are you from a System planet?" he asked suddenly.

I started, turning toward him and trying to keep my fear in check.

"I can tell by your accent," he smiled. "Don't worry, you've nothing to fear from me. What are you running from?"

"The System," I said simply.

"No need to worry about that here. This planet hasn't been System since the Special Knowledge was discovered. Now that the Separation is possible, we have no need of the System."

"But will they force us to be Separated?"

"No force, only subtle persuasion. Like I said, there's

no advancement open to me until I'm separated. But Separation is nothing to fear, they say."

"Then, why don't you do it?"

"I'm just not ready," he shrugged. "I keep hearing rumors about Colasse-City, what an exciting place it is. It just makes me wonder."

"Aren't the Colassenes and Nosticenes bitter enemies?"

"Oh yes. They're total opposites in all ways. Like fire and water. They don't have anything to do with each other, even to fight."

"Are you going to Colasse someday?" I wasn't sure why I asked this, but an idea was forming in my mind, that I should see what this opposite place was like.

"I think I just might," he smiled.

"Could I come with you, perhaps?"

"I thought you might ask," he laughed, slapping me on the back. "I was right about you. You'll love the liberty there."

I wasn't sure what to make of this comment, but right now this seemed to be our only way to get out of Urbis.

"Say," I added casually, "I have a friend at the infirmary I'd like to visit. Could you tell me the best way to get there?"

"Sure." He gave me the correct tube number on a small yellow token. "Just put that in the entry-stile, and you'll end up right there. Also, if you're really serious about Colasse, I think I'll try to get there in a week or two. You'll have to call me if you're still interested, unless you want to give me your number."

"I—uh—I'm not sure where I'll be."

"Here's my number," he smiled again, handing me a small red token with black marks on it. "Just put that in a tele-terminal, and it will connect you to me."

"Thanks, Kotam," I nodded, smiling at him. "You've been a real friend."

"Call me," he said.

***

"But can we trust him?" Martina repeated.

"I'm not sure," I admitted. "But I know we want to steer clear of this Separation business. And from what I've seen of Urbis, I really don't think we want to stay. It's the drabbest, most tasteless place I've ever seen."

"I thought this place was drab because it was a hospital, and the food was just institution food."

"Well, it's typical of the whole city," I grinned. "You don't want to spend the rest of your life like this, do you?"

"And you think their Separation Ceremony is just a hoax?"

I nodded. "It's engineered somehow with holograms. Maybe the Separated ones do achieve some sort of mind control over themselves, like some kind of hypnosis."

"We've tried stuff like that before, haven't we?" she

sighed. "On Pyrrhia and Sophian, both."

I drew her closer to me. "We won't fall for that trap again," I whispered. "They all seem to be offshoots of the System, whether they admit it or not."

"It sure seems like it," she agreed. "If the True Lord of the Universe is somewhere out there, I sure hope he's different. I hope he isn't just another incarnation of the System."

"Me, too." I sighed. "Otherwise, our search will be in vain."

"All I can go on is what Father taught us when we were young," she said. "He said the System was opposed to the True Lord, and though all the world would forsake him, we'd continue to be true to him, no matter what."

"But why doesn't anyone we meet seem to know anything about it?" I asked.

"That old man Johan knew something."

"Well, yes, he did. So maybe there *is* some hope," I admitted.

She drew closer to me, and I cradled her head against my shoulder.

"I'm just glad you're here with me," she whispered. Then after a long silence, she asked, "What shall we do about Jael?"

"You said he seemed better today?"

"I think so. He seems stronger, and once I thought I saw his eyelids twitch."

We were both looking down at the still form on the bed. He did look more peaceful lying there. Did I see a slight muscle movement in his face? Or was I only wishing it? Suddenly his little finger moved.

"Look!" cried Martina. She'd seen it too.

Ever so slowly, the little finger quivered and raised up from the bedclothes. Soon the next finger followed, and then the other three. His hand hung there, trembling in mid-air for an instant. Then Martina grabbed it.

"I'm here, Jael," she said hoarsely. "Can you hear me?"

There came another definite twitch of his eyelids, and suddenly his eyes were open. His mouth didn't seem to work too well, though. He opened it, but no words came out. Perhaps it was because of the breathing tubes. Then it seemed a smile played at his lips. He looked at his sister for a long time, as she held his hand against her cheek, saying softly over and over, "Welcome back, Jael. Welcome back."

Then his eyes turned to me, and I could see the light of recognition in them. "I knew you were a fighter," I whispered hoarsely to him.

The next morning, he was markedly improved. He had control of his hands and could speak a few simple words. The doctor was amazed when he saw him.

"He has a strong spirit," he observed.

"Yes sir," I nodded. "Soon his body will be strong again, too."

"We must schedule your Separations soon," he said quickly.

"We aren't sure about that yet, sir," I said cautiously. "Could we perhaps get our own place in the city first?"

His eyes flashed, taking my words as a challenge, but his voice betrayed no anger as he spoke again. "You don't know our world well," he said evenly. "Only menial workers are un-separated."

"Still, sir, we'd like a little more time to think about it."

"As you wish," he turned abruptly on his heel and left us.

"What will he do to us now?" Martina asked fearfully.

"He can't force us into Separation, according to Kotam," I said. "He'll only use all the persuasion he can. We must hold out."

'What is Separation?' came a once-familiar voice in my mind.

"Feier! You're awake, too!"

'Yes, I'm back from walking the dark pathways with Jael.'

"Is he going to be okay?" Martina asked.

'Oh yes. But it will take time.'

"Hey," came another small voice. "What are you all talking about?"

We turned to see hints of the old Jael in his eyes. My heart beat with new hope.

***

Over the next week, Jael grew stronger each day. In fact, his recovery was just short of a miracle. Even Rehoba had to admit that Jael's body was very resilient.

At last the day came when he could be detached from the breathing apparatus for a short time. Soon he was permitted short walks with us in the infirmary corridors, and later out on the grounds, where some of the few trees in Urbis were planted.

As we walked one sunny afternoon, I wondered about those trees. They seemed to be one slight surrender of the ascetic strictness of Urbis, a bit of beauty for the eyes of the sick. Yes, they were probably the ones who needed beauty most. I wondered if the trees had been allowed in a moment of weakness. Perhaps someone realized that if people didn't get well, they couldn't be convinced to become Separated.

I finally shrugged all this off, not sure I'd ever understand the mind of the Nosticenes. All I knew was their ways were not for me, that Urbis wasn't the right place for us. But should I call Kotam and ask him to take us to Colasse? I wasn't sure about that either.

A couple of days later, Rehoba grudgingly admitted that Jael could be released from the infirmary. "I can only place you in laborers' quarters," he said. "Until you agree to Separation, that is. And you must take emergency breathing apparatus for him."

He showed us how to use the equipment, and we agreed to take it.

"But what do we owe you for all this?" I asked. "How can we ever repay you?"

"It will be taken from your wages, as it is for all citizens," he said.

"But I don't have a job, yet," I said.

"I've found you a position at the firm which ships many of our medical supplies," he said, and I almost saw him smile.

"Really? I'm going to be forever in your debt," I gasped. "How can I ever repay you?"

"I think you already know," he smiled wider.

I did feel sorry then that I couldn't promise him we'd accept his Separation, but I knew deep down we never would. Instead I just took his hand, and to my surprise he returned my handshake.

***

Three or four weeks passed, with the three of us living in a small, drab flat in the heart of Urbis. It was very close to my work, which was a warehouse similar to the one where I'd met Kotam. I worked a morning shift the first couple of weeks, and once I thought I recognized the voices of the two drivers I'd hitched a ride with the day I sneaked out of the infirmary.

We didn't exactly settle into the domestic setting I hoped for, though. Martina now seemed totally absorbed in taking care of Jael and insisted on sleeping in his room instead of mine. After her begging forgiveness and telling me she really did love me, I was confused. She didn't act as angry as before, but there was no denying she seemed to be distancing herself from me again.

I wanted to talk to her about it, but there never seemed to be any right time. And I had a feeling I knew the truth; now Jael was back and she didn't need me as much as she thought before.

We were thankful for Rehoba's breathing apparatus, as Jael did have difficulties breathing at night. His rasping wheezes were very frightening, but gradually he coughed up much of the fluid accumulated in his lungs. Each night seemed a little better than the last.

I was amazed at how much Rehoba did for us, in spite of our stubbornness about his plan of Separation. It almost made me feel guilty. One morning I realized this was probably just what he was hoping for. He thought if I felt obligated enough to him I'd be persuaded to cooperate.

For the next couple of weeks, I was on a night shift, so I wasn't at the flat when the others were asleep. One early morning, though, they were still in bed when I came in. I was tired of walking on eggshells around Martina, and so without much thought, I just walked into their room. She was lying on a floor-mat next to Jael's bed, and I carefully slipped under the covers, lying beside her. She stirred slightly in her sleep, then rolled over, and her arm landed across my chest.

I decided to just lie there for awhile, pretending this was intentional on her part. When she still didn't wake, I gently turned to where I was facing her, and softly ran my fingers across her cheek and down her smooth, white neck. Perhaps she thought I was part of a dream, for a smile twitched her lips, and they puckered into a kiss as my hand touched them. I couldn't resist pulling her body closer to me, and still she slept. In fact, she snuggled against me and sighed contentedly.

But suddenly her breath came in a sharp gasp, and she pulled away from me. "What do you think you're doing?" she hissed.

I held her more tightly. "Martina, you know I love you. And you say you love me. Why can't we be as we once were? I really need you."

"Perhaps I do love you," she said, and now I could see tears beginning to trickle down her cheeks. "But I'm not worthy of your love. I'm nothing but an old used plaything. I want to be clean and beautiful for someone like you. Please, Jon."

I felt the old anger rising in me again. It was still the same old story she used over and over before. "I keep trying to understand why you feel this way," I muttered. "But it doesn't make sense to me. If we love each other, and we've already been together, why can't we make love, now that all we have is each other?"

"You just don't see, do you Jon? I need to be another person—a good person—and I can't seem to find out how to do it. I can't be with you like I was before. There's no way I can go back to being that person ever again."

By this time, she was sobbing in my arms.

"Shh, now," I whispered. "Don't wake Jael. Just let me hold you for a little while. That's all I'll do. I promise. Just let me fall asleep here beside you."

And so that's what we did. I was exhausted from my night's work, oblivious to the world very soon, anyway. But when I woke again, a few hours later, I was alone on the mat.

Thoughts crowded into my head as I lay there. "If only I could help her see how much I love her," I sighed to the empty room. "Johan talked about that fountain. If only we could find it! Maybe then I could convince Martina how committed I am now. I'm not the same person I was with the Redlarks, either. There's got to be a way to reach her."

✳✳✳

That day, I realized it was time to call Kotam. He now seemed to be our only way of getting out of Urbis, and I knew we couldn't stay there much longer. I also hoped a change of scene might help Martina open up to me again. So, after work the next morning, I went to a tele-com box and put in the token he'd given me.

"Yes?" came his familiar voice.

"This is Jo—Jakol," I said. "Are you still planning on going to Colasse?"

"You want to come?" his voice sounded excited.

"Yes, I do—and two friends, too."

"Three of you? That could be tricky."

"I can't go without them. One can't walk very well, either," I added. "He's been very ill."

"Are you sure you *all* want to go then?"

"We have no other choice, Kotam," I added, thinking to myself he had no idea what this really meant.

"All right. I'll see what I can do. Where can I meet you? Better make it tomorrow evening. I'll need the time to get a vehicle."

I told him the address of our flat.

The next day I spent on a rollercoaster of indecision. Was this too much of a gamble, trusting our fates to Kotam like this? I barely knew him or what he truly believed. But really, what other choice was there? No other way out of the city had presented itself.

I was back on day shift, so after I got home we ate an evening meal that was larger than usual—since we really didn't know when our next meal would be. We had few belongings to pack, so there was room for some preserved food Martina got for us. Besides, there was little left of our gear since the crash of our ship.

"What about this?" asked Martina, indicating the breathing apparatus.

"I can do without it," said Jael confidently.

'You shouldn't take chances,' Feier said.

"No, we should take it," I said. "You might relapse under the added stress of travel. I can handle the extra weight."

"Are you sure?" he asked.

"Hey, you're worth it, Little Brother," I smiled.

Martina gave me a warm smile, so I hoped maybe things would get better between us again.

We waited and watched as dusk fell and darkness settled over Urbis. 'Will Kotam come at all?' I began to wonder. 'Or will he report us to some authorities instead? Perhaps he's been a spy for them all along.'

Just as I was about to decide he forgot us, a rickety old truck pulled into the alley behind our flat. As the driver got out and stood casually by the cab, I recognized his face.

"There he is." I whispered. "Let's go."

Without much ado, we left the flat for the last time. Good-byes to places had ceased for us a long time ago in our wanderings, for we never settled in one place long enough to become attached. I was carrying the breathing apparatus, and since Jael was still too weak to carry Feier,

Martina settled him in the top of her pack-sack.

When we stepped to the truck, Kotam flashed his familiar smile. "So, you're ready for our adventure, eh?"

I nodded.

"And these are your friends?" he asked.

"Yes. This is Martina, My—uh…"

She finished for me, "Partner."

Kotam shrugged. "Okay. Just don't you cramp his style."

"No fears there," she smiled at him sweetly.

"You're full of surprises, Jakol," he said as I wondered what he meant by this.

"This is her brother, Jael," I added.

"Anyway," Kotam continued, "This is the best vehicle I could get on short notice. Anyone who stops us will think I'm just a farmer headed back to the country after making deliveries. Is this all the stuff you're taking? Not nearly as much as I expected. Some people take way too much."

"Oh, we travel light," Martina tried to laugh.

Kotam's words tapered off at the end, but I heard them. Had he made this trip before? Perhaps he had a business carting people to Colasse, and there was much more to him than I realized.

"Yes, this is all we need," I said then, pretending I hadn't noticed anything.

"That's good," he said. "Well, let's get going. We don't have all night."

We clambered into the back of the rickety truck. The side panels swayed but at least seemed solid enough to conceal us. Kotam unrolled a piece of heavy canvas to cover the back after we seated ourselves on the floor. As the pungent smell of the canvas and dirty wood began to fill our nostrils, Jael whispered hoarsely, "I'm glad you insisted on bringing the breathing apparatus."

"Me, too," I replied, squeezing his hand.

The truck gave a sudden lurch. 'Here we go on another adventure,' I heard Feier say in my mind.

Martina suddenly took my hand and squeezed it. I wasn't sure if she was seeking comfort or trying to give it. Perhaps both.

The truck rolled slowly through the night streets. We were leaving Urbis, entirely in Kotam's hands now.

For the rest of the night, the truck lurched slowly over bumpy rural roads. We all dozed off and on, and Jael used his breathing apparatus most of the night.

As a chill dawn began to lighten around the edges of the canvas, we huddled together for warmth. I realized I had no idea how far Colasse was, or even whether Kotam was taking us in the right direction. The day wore on, and the truck never stopped, except once, when he handed us some crusty bread and a jug of water.

"I'm sorry, that's all I have," he grinned. "But you'll find the fare much better in Colasse."

There it was again, hints that he'd made this trip before.

He wouldn't let us out of the truck, lest we be seen. "I have to keep up the appearance of a poor farmer wending his way home from the city," he explained.

"When will we get to Colasse?" I finally asked, just before he closed the canvas again.

"About nightfall tonight," he said. Then he grinned suddenly, "Just in time for the orgy."

The canvas dropped, and so did my jaw.

"Orgy?" Martina hissed. "What are we getting ourselves into?"

"I don't know," I whispered back. "I guess I should've suspected something, if they're the exact opposite of the Nosticenes. While everything in Urbis is drab and gray, Colasse must be the place where anything goes."

"Like the Underground, huh?" she nodded.

"I guess we'll find out soon enough," I sighed.

"But are we ready for it?"

"You know, Jon," said Jael softly, "I get the feeling Kotam has done this sort of thing before."

"Yes, I think so, too." I nodded. "He isn't just a Nosticene who's curious to see Colasse, as he first led me to believe. I think he's a Colassene sent to Urbis to lure people away to Colasse."

"So perhaps he's lured us into a trap." moaned Martina.

"Well, we're out of Urbis anyway." I tried to sound upbeat. "Perhaps Colasse won't be all that bad."

"I just wish we could get off this planet," whispered Jael.

'We need a ship for that,' Feier added, stating the obvious.

"I'll find a way somehow," I muttered, hoping I could make those words come true.

CHAPTER 14

THE OPPOSING SIDE

Unfortunately, Colasse turned out to be almost as bad as we feared. As we neared the city, we could hear raucous shouts and a wild sort of dancing music. The familiar smells and sounds of the Terres Underground assaulted my senses.

We drove quite a way into the city, with the sounds of the orgy getting nearer all the while, until at last the truck stopped.

"This is my place," Kotam said as he helped us out. "Come inside and rest up before the fun begins."

I had to confront him. "So you *are* a Colassene?"

"Yes, I'm sorry I had to deceive you. It's the best way to work in Urbis, I've found."

"We aren't Nosticenes. We have no prejudices about Colasse."

"Are you sure, Jakol?" He looked directly into my eyes.

I found I couldn't answer.

"Come inside for a bit." He opened a small door. "You're welcome to my flat."

Once we were safely inside, I asked, "What is this orgy business?"

"They'll be here soon, and then you'll see," he smiled.

"I think I already know," said Martina stiffly.

"Our home planet of Terres had an Underground that was like this."

"Well, you'll find there's no resisting here." He drew uncomfortably close to Martina as he said this. "You'll be caught up in the aura of the air-drugs, and then nothing will matter."

"Air drugs?" we asked together.

"Mass narcotics. They help us all relax so we can really enjoy ourselves—and our neighbors."

I reached over and pulled Martina closer to me. "But why?"

"Why not?" he shrugged. "It doesn't matter. Pleasure is good. And it does no harm."

"Are you sure about that?" Martina hissed.

"Of course, my dear. We've discovered what the Nosticenes missed. The body can be free of the spirit just as well as the spirit can be free from the body. They're total opposites, so whatever we do with our bodies does no harm to our spirit."

This was the complete antithesis of Urbis, and I could

tell Kotam really believed what he was saying. Those air drugs must have a tremendous impact on thought processes. And I realized then we were trapped. We'd escaped Separation in Urbis, only to face the all-encompassing air drugs of Colasse. And I'd brought us here.

"But what about Jael?" Martina's question jarred me back into the present.

"He's been very ill," I cut in quickly. "He's not up to anything too—uh, strenuous."

"No worry," he sighed. "I can give him a sedative to counteract the air drugs. Then he'll just sleep through it all, though I can't guarantee he won't dream."

"Do it, then!" Martina snapped.

He took a small vial off a shelf above the sink. "I use this when I prepare myself to return to Urbis. I must sleep out at least two orgies before I return. Don't worry, it's safe. I said I use it myself, didn't I?" He was glancing at Martina as he said this.

"Go ahead and take it, Jael," I nodded. Kotam showed him the proper dose for his size. Soon Jael was yawning, and lay down on a cushion near the wall.

I was beginning to feel fuzzy around the edges and realized the air drugs must be beginning to reach us. When I closed my eyes, I saw that all-too-familiar red glow I'd seen in the Underground. Then I opened them and was shocked to see Kotam with his arms around Martina, trying to kiss her.

"Hey, she's mine!"

"Yours, mine, ours?" he laughed. "What does it matter?"

"She's mine," I repeated, pulling her towards me.

"Oh, all right. You can have her first. I'll go get one of my own. Maybe when you see mine, you'll want to trade."

I could feel Martina shuddering as I held her close to me. "We've got to concentrate on each other. It's the only way we'll get through this night."

"I love you, Jon," she murmured into my ear, through my hair. I found myself hoping this wasn't just the drugs speaking. As the door closed behind Kotam, I drew her closer and soon the red heat of passion engulfed both of us.

***

I woke slowly, as though from a long restless sleep. My mind began to move around the room before my body would budge. I spoke to Kotam, or thought I did. But when I finally got my eyes open, I saw him still lying asleep on the floor nearby. He seemed to be in a sort of stupor.

Martina was next to me on the bed where I lay. I wondered what happened after the air drugs hit us full force. But I had no distinct memories, only a warm sense of pleasure just past. These air drugs were certainly powerful—and dangerous.

At least Jael escaped this time. I wondered if these

orgies were a nightly occurrence and sincerely hoped they weren't. I had to find a way out of Colasse as soon as possible, to keep from being swallowed entirely in this culture of 'anything-goes'.

Already, I could feel a part of me saying, 'Why should we leave? There's great pleasure here, and it hurts no one. Can it be so wrong? You don't feel any guilt, do you?'

No, I didn't feel guilty. I couldn't even remember what had happened. But I did feel an angry tightening in my throat, as I wondered whether Kotam found a way to carry out his plan of trading another girl for Martina.

Just then, she stirred beside me. "Jon?" Her voice was groggy and full of sleep.

"I'm right here."

"What happened?"

"I'm not sure." I tried to smile into her eyes. "I guess they leave it to our imaginations." This was better than telling her my worst fears, I hoped.

"I feel so tired, but sort of pleased."

"Me, too. It's the drugs, I think."

"How's Jael?" There was sudden concern in her voice.

"Still sleeping." I nodded toward the cushion where his small form lay curled, just as it was the last I saw him. Feier was nestled close beside him. "I don't think Feier will let any harm come to him."

She suddenly grabbed my hand tightly. "Jon, we've got to get out of this place."

"I know."

"But how?"

"I'll figure out something." I tried to sound reassuring.

"You always seem to come through." She planted a quick kiss on my lips. I hoped this wasn't just a hang-over from the drugs.

Later that day, after we had a meal, and Kotam seemed in a talkative mood, I decided to find some answers.

"How often are the orgies?" I tried to sound as casual as I could.

"Every seventh day. There's some significance to the seventh day in The Book, I think."

"The seventh day is given to mankind as a day of rest," said Jael. "It says so here, 'And God blessed the seventh day and made it holy, because on it he rested from all the work of creating that he had done'."

"Jael, how do you always find those passages that fit every situation?" I asked.

He just shrugged and smiled slightly. "I study it every day."

"So you see, we're right in tune with The Book," said Kotam lightly.

Personally, I had my doubts whether God meant the day of rest to be an orgy, but right then I didn't think it would help to mention this. "We're just trying to let The Book be our guide," was all I said.

"Then you should like it here," Kotam smiled.

"Do you have a job in Colasse?"

"Oh yes, Jakol. I work at the spaceport when I'm here. They're used to people coming and going there."

"You mean there are space flights from here?"

"Of course. The Nosticenes have little use for such things, being too wrapped up in themselves, and not wanting any beauty or frills in their lives. But we Colassenes are much more progressive. We trade in all sorts of luxuries, and we even have ships that can cross the GAP."

"Really?" I tried to sound as casual as I could. "Do you think I could come to work with you sometime?"

"I don't see why not. They might even have an opening for a laborer somewhere."

I returned his friendly smile, but all the while my heart was pounding. Perhaps I could find a way out for us, after all. Maybe we could even get away before the next orgy.

***

The next few days passed much too quickly, as we went about our daily tasks. I went to work with Kotam and was able to begin a job there in the cargo loading area. I hoped we could find a way to stow-away in the cargo hold of a ship. But first, I had to find out whether these holds were pressurized and oxygenated. Otherwise we might as well be drifting bodily in open space.

I soon learned most of the basic cargo ships were left in space-vacuum, which would be an impossible environment to survive without special suits. My hopes began to fade for an early escape. In fact, another orgy came and went, which we endured as we did the one before. This only made me all the more anxious to avoid another.

Though he'd been awake when we left Urbis, Feier now seemed to be in a constant state of sleep. Jael was worried but told us Feier assured him this was a normal part of his life cycle. Most of the time, I forgot about him, but once in awhile I would see his furry form curled up in a corner somewhere, and then I'd wonder what was going on in that little body.

Kotam didn't sense anything wrong with our attitudes, as far as I could tell. We did our best to make him believe we wanted to stay in Colasse. It was easy to convince him we didn't want to go back to Urbis, at any rate.

"You can stay with me as long as you like," he said. "Martina is a good cook."

When he said this, I shuddered, for I knew he wanted her around for the next orgy.

"We do appreciate your help," I said. "All the same, we'll probably try to find our own place soon." What I didn't add was we hoped this place would be off the planet.

Once I heard him refer to his planet as 'Terra.'

"Where does that name come from, Kotam? I thought this was Platius."

"Terra is one of the names of the original home planet of humans," he replied. "Like scattered settlers in many places, our ancestors named this place after their home, and called it Terra. The System is who called us Platius."

"So the original home planet *was* called Terra, or Earth. I heard stories about it. Maybe that's why *our* planet was called Terres. Do you have any records of where this home planet might be found?"

"Unfortunately, they've been lost."

I felt my heart sink. "How do you know this?"

"Oh, I searched for them many times," he sighed. "Didn't your planet have any records, either?"

"I think the System doesn't want to admit there was a time when they didn't exist, a time when mankind wasn't interplanetary." I decided to try one more name for Earth. "Have you ever heard of a planet called Maia?"

Kotam shrugged. "Sorry. Never heard of it."

***

Finally, my luck changed for the better just two days before the next orgy. A great excitement was running through the whole spaceport that day. We were to prepare to load troop ships the next evening, and troop ships had pressurized cargo bays. Hope at last for potential stowaways!

"There's going to be a great battle in the Centauri Sector, they think," someone told me. "The Rebels are preparing an assault, it's believed."

"Centauri Sector?" I asked. Hadn't Johan mentioned that place?

"Who knows why those Rebels go where they do? Or where they get any support, even. Still, we've been asked to send reinforcements."

"For the Rebels?"

"Are you kidding? How can anyone support the Rebels, with the power the System has? You'd think they would've been cut off years ago."

"Aren't there some Rebels on this planet?" I tried to ask as casually as I could.

"They get no support from Colasse!" He said this sharply, as though I were a System agent testing his loyalty. "I've no idea how they get support."

As we continued with our work, I began to wonder about this, too. Who were these Rebels, anyway? They were said to be in opposition to the System—which we were fleeing. Yet we'd never found any of them, much less tried to join them. They seemed to have few allies, not even the liberal Colassenes. How could they be strong enough to launch an attack in Centauri Sector?

Soon, however, I forgot these musings in my excitement about the troop ships. There were even going to be supply ships with pressurized holds, which would have fewer crew members on board to contend with. As soon as I learned this, it didn't take me long to formulate a plan. And that night, at the apartment was the perfect opportunity to tell the others, for Kotam was out working late.

"But is Jael ready for space travel?" Martina asked.

Before I could answer her, I could see him nodding vigorously. "But how do we get them to let us on?"

"We won't give them a chance to stop us," I smiled at him. "We'll just stowaway on a ship. Troop ships, and their supply ships, have pressurized holds, so we won't need any special equipment. And the best part is they're heading to the Centauri Sector."

"Isn't that where Johan said Maia is?" Jael asked.

"I think so," I nodded.

"When should we do this?" whispered Martina.

"I think it should be tonight. Final loading is scheduled for tomorrow, and we'd best be on board before that. I think I have just the plan to get us all on."

That evening, before Kotam even got home, we gathered our few belongings.

"I keep feeling like we should thank Kotam for his help," mused Jael.

"I know how you feel. But I don't think he'd understand our wanting to leave so soon. And we don't really want him to know what we're doing." What I didn't add, was that we needed to be gone before the next orgy, something Jael hadn't experienced, fortunately for him.

"If only Kotam would come with us to seek the truth," Jael continued.

"I hadn't really thought of it that way," Martina added. "He is just lost and searching, like we are. He doesn't know right from wrong."

"We're still searching, too. We haven't found many answers yet." Jael was helping Feier into his pack-sack.

"Yeah, just a lot of 'unanswers'," she sighed.

"That's why we must keep moving on," I said. "I'm afraid Kotam would just think us foolish. Come on—we need to get going."

***

We were almost there now, Martina and I, dressed in our laborers' coveralls and carrying the cargo box between us that held Jael and Feier. We'd even managed to fit in his emergency breathing apparatus. He hadn't needed it for several days now, but we'd included it in case the stress of liftoff became too much for him.

The box was more awkward than heavy, because it was on suspension wheels. At last we entered the hold. This time of night, there weren't many other workers around. We were dressed like the few we did see, and no one seemed to notice our presence. In another stroke of luck, we found a supply ship scheduled for take-off within an hour, so we wouldn't have to make ourselves inconspicuous for so long.

Once we had the box secured in its berth, I glanced around for a place to hide. There were several other boxes lined up beyond ours, and we tried to crouch behind them. I heaved a sigh of relief as the lights began to dim in preparation for liftoff.

Suddenly the box next to me opened, and two lithe forms slipped out. The strange insignia on their sleeves, a sunburst with something looking like a plus-sign, made me wonder if they were Rebels. Evidently someone else also had my idea about cargo boxes. This really put a kink in my plans!

I tried to slink back into the darker shadows. The last thing we needed, I thought, was to be Rebel hostages.

"What do you think you're doing?" a voice hissed suddenly in my ear.

Before I could reply, two hands grabbed my arms in an iron grip.

"Sir," the voice behind me said, "Some flunky sneaking around here."

"Here's another one!" a second voice called nearby.

My heart sank, as I saw another Rebel shove Martina toward me.

A dark-haired man, who evidently was 'Sir' stepped in front of me, his green eyes seeming to pierce right through me. Those eyes flashed even more brightly as he turned to Martina, and I shuddered. Her face paled suddenly at the sight of him, as though she was seeing a ghost.

Evidently the Rebel leader decided not to let us distract him from his current work, however. He motioned for our captors to put us in the cargo box behind him.

"We'll deal with them once we're in space. They can't go far, anyway. We've got to be quick now, while Skor can impress his image on the controls."

'So they have a firstborn with them,' I noted. 'Perhaps my ability can be an advantage to us later.'

But right then, we were being stuffed into a cargo box, and it was a tight fit for two of us. I tried to shift my weight off Martina, as she groaned. It was most comfortable, we found, to wrap our arms around each other. Then I heard a hiss as the lid sealed.

"I hope Jael is all right, all alone," she breathed in my ear.

"He has his respirator, and Feier is with him. Don't worry."

"It doesn't do much good to tell me that, Jon. I'm scared!"

"I won't let that Rebel leader hurt you. You're mine to defend, you know."

"Thanks, Jon." Her lips brushed at my cheek. "You know it's probably just my imagination, but for a second the leader looked a little familiar."

"I don't see how either of us could know any Rebels," I said. "We've never had any contact with these mysterious people."

I was trying to decide whether to say anything else to her, when I felt the ship shudder in the process of crossing the first GAP. We were headed into space. But who was guiding this ship, the Rebels or the Colassenes? And where were we going?

CHAPTER 15

IN REBEL HANDS

The answer to my question came when the lid was again lifted from our cargo box, and the faces of the two Rebels appeared.

"All right, you two. Get out! We're to take you to the brig with the rest of your countrymen."

"Countrymen?" Martina began.

'So they think we're Colassenes, too,' I thought.

They were binding us, when Martina suddenly cried, "Wait! There's someone else! In that cargo box."

"What are you doing?" I hissed at her.

"We can't leave Jael down here alone."

By this time, they took the lid off his box, and Feier leaped toward them, wings extended.

'Wait, Feier!' I told him. 'Better just stay calm for Jael's sake.'

The feier-cat came and stood obediently beside us, and the Rebels let him be, though they kept close eyes on him. Then I saw them lifting Jael out of the box. His face was pale, but he managed a weak smile at us.

"Jael," his sister cried, "Are you all right?"

The Rebels weren't as rough with him as I'd expected. In fact, they helped him over to my side and let him lean against me for support.

"I'll be okay," he whispered to us. "Just got dizzy in there."

Then I noticed the two Rebels were having a brief whispered conversation.

"What are you doing here?" one asked, turning to me.

I decided the truth was a good start. "We're stowaways."

"Aren't you Colassenes?"

"No, we're—uh—refugees."

"Refugees from where?"

I took a deep breath, knowing I was committed to our true story now. "Originally from planet Terres."

Then I saw their eyes growing wider in surprise. 'What have I done now?' I wondered.

"That means we take them to Dare," one whispered, and the other nodded.

"Come with us," he said gruffly.

They led us through a maze of corridors, ultimately entering the central control core of the ship. As I'd already deduced, the Rebels were in control of the ship, but apparently with a bare-bones crew. I'd counted ten of them so far.

"We're still with the Colassene convoy, sir," the one at the control panel said. "So far, they don't appear to suspect anything."

This was encouraging news to me. At least we were still heading for Centauri Sector.

Now one of our guards stepped up to the one who appeared to be the leader. The dark-haired man nodded and glanced our way, and again I saw those dark green eyes flash. He motioned for the guards to bring us closer to him, and then led us all into one of the compartments off the central core of the ship.

He seated himself in a comfortable-looking armchair, as we were brought in. "You may wait outside," he told the guards.

"Both of us, sir?"

"Yes!" he snapped. "Did I say otherwise?"

Both men appeared confused as they hurried out the door.

After it hissed closed, the leader stood and motioned for us all to be seated in a circular area nearby. Could this be normal questioning procedure? What was he up to?

"So, you say you're refugees from Terres?" he began, sounding casual. "It's been a long time since I was there. How are things?"

"We don't really know, sir," I said. "It's been a long time since we left, too."

"Were you there when the double-star came?"

"Yes." Jael jumped in before I could stop him. "We

had to flee the city. It was all burning. Jon helped me find Martina because she went to the Redlarks."

"And is this Martina?" He turned to look at her, then back to Jael. "So what is your name, young man?"

"Jael."

"And this older fellow?"

"He's Jon," said Jael.

There was an undercurrent of tension in the room that I didn't understand.

"And did you leave Terres as stowaways, too?"

'How perceptive he is,' I heard Feier thinking.

"No, sir." I admitted. "I piloted a ship, we—uh—stole."

"Ah!" he smiled. "A Rebel couldn't have said it better. You must be firstborn, then."

I nodded. That was my best card, and now it was played.

"And these have been your companions on the entire journey?" He swept his arm to indicate the others.

"Yes, Jael and I have been together since we fled Terres-City. Oh, and his feier-cat, too. Jael is my little brother."

His eyes lit up in surprise at this, and I wondered why.

"By blood relationship?" he asked sharply.

"No—just by friendship and shared trials."

The light in his eyes softened, and then he turned toward Martina. "Is she your wife then?" he asked.

"Well, we've been partners, in a way, since we left the Redlarks."

"We're still working on it," Martina said softly.

The Rebel leader's eyes went dark, and he said nothing for a few moments. "Where have you been in your travels?" He was looking at Martina intently.

"We've been so many places," she began. "But tried to stay away from System planets since we were arrested on Fatina. We escaped with help from a guard there, and went to Pyrrhia, where we tried to live the meditative lifestyle, but just couldn't. So, we kept wandering from place to place, but never seemed to find answers about the True Lord of the Universe. Then our ship crashed on Platius. Jael is still recovering."

"Is he better now?" he asked suddenly.

"Yes," she nodded. "He's improving, and we're trying to continue our search. We didn't like the lifestyles on Platius."

"And what are you seeking?" he asked, seeming to become more agitated.

"We're seeking the truth," I began.

"And peace of mind."

"And the True Lord of the Universe." Jael added softly.

"We're also looking for our brother, Darien," Martina said suddenly, looking directly at him.

Now I could distinctly see something shining in the corners of his eyes. He rose abruptly and turned away from us.

"He joined the Inland Raiders," she continued. "He was like us. He wanted to find the truth, and peace of mind, too. I see that now. I didn't understand him before, and I was wrong to treat him the way I did. If only I could see him again, I'd try to explain." Tears were streaming down her cheeks now. "I'd tell him how much I've learned about love. I'd tell him that I love him—just as much as I loved our brother Stephen."

I couldn't believe what I was seeing. Everything was like a waking dream. The man's shoulders were shaking, as sobs racked his body. Martina was on her feet now, walking slowly toward him. Jael stood and stared at the two of them, as though he was trying to wake from a dream.

"Dare," he mouthed. "They said their leader was 'Dare'."

The man turned toward us then, and in that instant, I saw the resemblance between him and Martina, as though he dropped a mask.

"Oh, Darien, we've found you at last!" She threw her arms around him.

"I didn't think you'd even want to find me," he murmured into her hair. Then he stepped back. "I suspected it was you from the time they brought you up. But I wanted to give you a choice not to claim me. I didn't want to force myself on you."

"Of course we claim you, Darien," she sobbed. "I was afraid you wouldn't claim us."

"Well, I do." He pulled her into a strong embrace. Then, releasing her, he turned to Jael. "So, this is my little brother." He held out his hand to him. "How you've grown!"

Jael ran to embrace him.

"And your companion is Jon. "I can see he cares a lot for both of you. You've been in good hands."

I nodded, feeling embarrassed, but glad he accepted me, too.

"You must be hungry." He motioned for us all to sit. "I'll arrange some quarters for you. We'll be in space awhile yet before the fun begins."

Now he called the guards and gave instructions for meals to be brought. Martina was gripping my hand. "I knew it from the first, I think. I don't understand how we can be so lucky. Those supernatural forces must be working that have helped us before."

As we sat eating our meal, Darien seemed to finally relax. "I have one more question. Who is this?" He was pointing at Feier.

"This is my feier-cat," Jael replied. "He can talk to us in our minds."

"Telepathy?" Darien seemed very surprised.

"Yes, he's helped me many times," Jael added. "And Jon, too. Feier was the one who brought us together. Martina can even hear him now."

"Where did you get him?"

"Raina, Jason's sister, gave him to me." Jael's voice broke off at the mention of his lost friend.

"I remember Jason," said Darien, but he wasn't

smiling. "Where do these creatures come from?"

"They live in the wilds of Terres," Martina said, changing the subject. "Now may I ask you a question?"

"Yes, of course," he smiled.

"How did you become a Rebel, and why?"

'Martina never beats around the bush,' Feier said.

Fortunately, Darien didn't seem uneasy at her question. Perhaps he was not worried about blowing a cover, anyway.

"As an Inland Raider," he began, "I was assigned to infiltrate the Rebel enclave on Platius."

"So you've been right there on Platius all this time?"

"Yes, but let me tell it. As you yourself said, I was seeking more than work when I joined the Raiders. I wanted to know the truth about all the things Father and Stephen taught us. Like—who is the True King? And what does he have to do with us now? I think I knew all along that he wasn't in the System, though I didn't want to believe it at first. But soon after I'd begun meeting with the Rebels, I began to realize what they were really rebelling against— and who they were for."

"They seem to be against everything and everyone else," she said.

"Well, mostly we're against the System."

"But the Colassenes and Nosticenes aren't in the System, and the Rebels are against them," Jael added.

"Well the Colassenes and Nosticenes aren't followers of the True Lord, either," I said. "They think they have their own revelation."

"That's just heresy."

"Heresy is a strong word, Darien," I said. "It implies you think you've found absolute truth."

He was looking me right in the eyes now. "I know who the True Lord of the Universe is, and I'm one of his servants. The so-called Rebels are his only true followers. In a sense, all the rest of the worlds are the ones in rebellion—against him. So you see, I've finally taken my stand and joined the Rebels."

We all sat silent at the power of his words. I found myself wanting to believe him, but wasn't sure I could. It would mean taking sides in the conflict, saying once and for all, 'This is right, and everything else is wrong.' Was I ready for this?

I looked up to find his eyes on me. "I know what you're thinking, Jon. It's hard to take sides, to put everything else behind you."

'How can he know what I'm thinking? Are you talking to him, Feier?'

'No, Jon,' came the immediate reply in my mind. 'He's just very perceptive, I think.'

"I know the System isn't right," I said cautiously. "And we haven't found any other place or person that can direct us to the Lord of the Universe."

"Except Johan."

"Right, Martina. Johan did tell us to look for Maia in Centauri Sector. But so far, no one seems to know where it is. It's not on any charts."

"That's exactly where we are taking this ship," said Darien evenly.

"You are? Why?"

"Well, Jael," Darien smiled at his younger brother, "The time has come for the final battle. We're going to take our stand for the King."

He looked directly at me then. As I tried to think of a response, the door suddenly hissed open. "Sir, the Colassenes have contacted us. They suspect something is wrong!"

Darien jumped up, assuming his leadership role in an instant. "Let them stay here in my quarters," he indicated Jael, Martina, and Feier. "Jon will come with me."

The guard registered some surprise at this last order but made no protest. I was certainly surprised. What did Darien have in mind for me?

In a matter of seconds, we were in the control room. A voice was coming over the transceiver: "C-201 transport, please acknowledge. Commander Tran, are you there?"

"There's no way we can respond without arousing suspicion, sir," the Rebel at the communications station whispered to Darien.

"Can you take evasive action, Skor?" Darien turned

to the man at the control console.

"I can try, but they may be able to track me, sir."

"Well, try it!" Darien hissed. "Take an unexpected direction across the GAP."

I saw Skor place his hands on the control arms and close his eyes. Then I felt the shudder that only a firstborn can feel, as we leaped across the GAP.

"They're tracking me, sir," the pilot said tensely. "They've been able to deduce my pattern."

"Jon, if we were to change pilots, could they track then?"

"Not as well," I said. "Especially if they'd never seen the new pilot's pattern."

"Then, get over there, Jon," he ordered. "You're the only other firstborn we've got right now."

Now I knew at least part of his plans for me.

"Take us away from the Centauri Sector, but not too far. Skor, let Jon take over."

Skor looked up in disbelief, but obeyed his commander.

As I took the controls, I suddenly thought. 'I'm in control now. I could take us anywhere.' But I also knew I couldn't risk Jael and Martina by doing something foolish. I took a quick glance at the chart, and decided to head for a small yellow star marked Sol. It appeared to be some four or five light-years from Alpha Centauri, a non-descript place. I took the crossing.

As we came out of the GAP, I opened my eyes again

and saw a large ringed planet pass by our viewer. A huge gaseous giant loomed ahead of us, and I adjusted a path to avoid its massive gravity. As we slipped by, I let our speed drop to sub-light. Then I saw Darien staring at me.

"No pursuers, are there?" I asked.

He shook his head. "How did you know?"

"Know what?"

"You have us on a direct course for Maia."

"I do?"

"Why did you choose this crossing?"

"It just looked like a nondescript area. I figured the least likely place they'd look was on the other side of the Centauri Sector."

"Well, you were right. You're headed for the lost planet that isn't even on the charts, to old Earth, the home of humankind. You'd make a great Rebel pilot, Jon."

I just nodded. It seemed unbelievable that I'd found our long-sought goal just by chance. But I wasn't sure I was ready to join the Rebels, or whether Darien was really offering me the choice.

"Skor, you take over now," he said crisply. "Jon, come with me."

We didn't go back to his quarters, as I'd expected, but up to the observation dome.

"Well, Jon, are you ready to join us, or not?"

I was surprised at how quickly this man came to the point. He seemed to be a person who made snap decisions.

"What do you want me to do?" I asked cautiously.

"To swear loyalty to the True King, Lord of the Universe."

"How can I, when I haven't even met him?"

"'He who is not for me, is against me,' he says in The Book."

"The Book?"

"Do you know it?"

"Johan gave us one. It has been a great help to us in our travels, though Jael is the one who reads it the most."

"Somehow that doesn't surprise me," he smiled. "You know The Book is the word of the Lord?"

"It does seem to have a power beyond any other book I've ever read."

"So you've read other books, too? Sometimes it seemed my family were the only ones left who did."

"Yes, Martina and Jael told me."

"Now will you swear loyalty to the King?"

"I can't yet." I looked him straight in the eyes. "Please try to understand. We've been to many planets and found many deceptions. Many religious people claimed to have the truth, and only later did we see the lies hiding in the fine-sounding words. It's hard to know the truth, without studying *all* the facts."

His eyes glowed in what seemed to be anger for an instant, but suddenly they softened. "You remind me of myself. I remember how it was to have a desperate need to be sure. I'll take you back to my brother and sister. Perhaps you can talk it over. But each one must decide for him or herself."

I nodded and followed him toward the door. As we were about to leave, I saw a tiny blue planet, speckled with white clouds, coming into view.

"What's that? Do you know its name?"

"Don't you know, Jon? That's Maia, the mother planet of all humanity. In ancient times, when it was the only planet we lived on, it was called Earth—or Terra."

"But it seems to be mostly ocean. They should have called it Oceania instead."

"Interesting, isn't it? When it was named, no one had even sailed all those oceans, let alone seen it from space."

No one had seen it from space? How long ago that must have been! I couldn't even fathom that length of time.

"How do you know so much about this planet, when no one else does?"

"It's the place where the True King dwells. Didn't you know?"

I took a step back in surprise. "On this little planet? But why isn't it on the charts?"

"All those in rebellion against him have cut themselves off. He's let them go in their ignorance—until now. So they either don't know where he is or refuse to know, and so Maia has become lost to all but the Rebels, his true followers."

'And yet, I put us on course for it, unknowingly,' I thought to myself. 'Incredible! That strange force which guided me before—could it be this Lord?'

"Come, Jon." He interrupted my thoughts. "I must take you back to the others."

***

"I think we can trust Darien," Jael was saying.

"Yes," Martina nodded.

"You can say that because he's your brother. But how do we *know* that all this is the truth?" I asked her.

"By faith, I guess."

"That's what The Book says, 'We walk by faith, not by sight.' It's right here." Jael had The Book open across his lap. The way his eyes shone as he read reminded me again how this Book did have some unique power.

Each time we'd been at a crisis in our journey, words from The Book were the key unlocking the answer for us. We owed that to Jael's diligence in reading it, I knew. 'I should study it more myself,' I thought.

"Darien said The Book is the words of the King of the Universe," I mused aloud.

"It certainly has great power," she agreed.

"I think Darien is right," Jael nodded. "I just feel it somehow, deep within me. And his story about Maia agrees with Johan's. No one else we've met has even come close."

I nodded. "All that is true." They both were looking at me expectantly—no, looking *to* me was more like it. They still saw me as their leader and guide in our journey. But how could I show the way when I didn't know it?

"I'm sorry. I guess I'm a doubter by nature, you guys."

"Doubts aren't all bad," said Jael, flipping to a new section in The Book.

'Doubts make us even more diligent in seeking the truth,' Feier said.

"You always know just what to say, don't you, Feier?" Martina added.

"There are doubters in The Book, too," said Jael. "Here's the story of one called Thomas. He doubted the Lord's resurrection, until he could see the Lord's body for himself, and touch it."

"What resurrection?" I asked.

"Back when the Lord first came to Earth as a man, he was killed by the unbelievers, but three days later he rose from the dead."

"Rose from the dead? That's impossible!" I cried.

"That's exactly what Thomas said," nodded Jael, unperturbed at my outburst. "Then the Lord came and showed himself to Thomas personally. He let Thomas touch him, to show he was real."

"I guess that's the kind of proof I'd need, too."

"Listen to what the Lord said to Thomas, 'Blessed are they who have not seen and yet believe'."

I could feel those words gripping me in the gut. What was the power of this Book? Was it related to the power which had guided us in unexpected directions when we needed it most? Like now, when we were heading for Maia, the very place where all these events supposedly happened?

I shook my head. "I guess I *am* like Thomas. I want to believe, but it seems I just can't."

"Perhaps going to Maia will help," said a voice behind me.

I turned in surprise to see Darien standing in the doorway. How long had he been there?

"Yes," Jael was saying. "That's where we need to go. Johan told us to find Maia."

Darien smiled at him. "I can see you're as perceptive as we thought when you were small. And you've really studied The Book, too. That's excellent. You're just the person I need to help me with my mission to Maia."

"I am?" Jael sounded thrilled.

"What mission?" I asked, trying not to let my suspicions show in my voice.

"Reconnaissance," he replied. "Our contingent hasn't been to Maia for a long time, as Earth time is measured."

"Earth time? What's the difference?" asked Martina.

"Each planet has its own rate of rotation and revolution," I said.

"It's more than that, though. Haven't you heard of the Theory of Relativity?" Darien asked.

Martina shook her head, but I nodded. Somewhere back in my schooling, I remembered, "Time doesn't always pass at the same rate," I murmured.

"That's the gist of it," Darien nodded. "As your velocity increases toward the speed of light, the passage of time decreases. A person crossing the GAP may experience five minutes, while on a planet traveling at normal speed, the time may be a year or more."

"Gosh!" cried Jael. "How long have we been out here wandering in Earth time?"

"A very long time," Darien said. "I'd need a computer to calculate it."

"Isn't there a way to compensate for the time difference?" I asked. "How can planets communicate? How can the System function?"

"The System has the secret of compensation," Darien added. "Non-system planets live in the isolation of their own time, with little or no outside contact."

"That's why all the non-System planets we visited seemed to just run on their own times. But what about the Rebels? What do you do?"

"Our calculations aren't as sophisticated as the System's. We do our best, but there's a greater margin of error."

"Thus, the need for reconnaissance on Earth," I said.

Darien nodded. "We must learn exactly what the status of Earth is now. Then we'll know if our calculations are correct for the great battle."

'The time secret,' I was musing to myself. 'I must learn that secret somehow.' This thought excited me beyond words. It was as though destiny had tapped me on the shoulder.

"Will you come with me, Jael?" I heard Darien ask.

"He can't go alone!" Martina cried.

"Don't you trust your own brother?" Darien's voice turned sharp. I could see he did have a very quick temper, though he controlled it most of the time. Then I thought of Martina's moods, and decided it must run in the family.

"I think she means we'd all like to go to Maia," I said. "After all, it's the very place we've been seeking for so long."

Darien nodded, "I'm willing to take all of you. We can go disguised as pilgrims to the home planet."

He was smiling, and I realized this was his idea all along. Had he just been testing our loyalty to Jael?

"Why do we need to go disguised?" I asked. "I thought you said Maia was lost to all but the Rebels?"

"Yes, but we still must be careful. Even within Rebel ranks there are those who waver and stray from the faith."

'Threats on every side,' I thought. 'This confirms I was correct to continue in my doubts. Caution is the key.'

"We'll come with you, Darien," I said aloud, once again speaking for our group.

"Good. Now we must go to our briefing. Your clothing is suitable as it is. I'll need to get out of this uniform, though."

***

The briefing was over now, and we were sealed into the shuttle pod. In only a few minutes, we'd be headed for the surface of this mysterious planet, Maia—or Earth, as Darien called it.

In fact, he'd warned us to start calling it 'Earth' if we wanted to be convincing as pilgrims. 'Earth,' I said to myself. 'Such a simple word. Synonym for soil, ground, dust. The place from which we came.'

Earlier, Jael read to us words from The Book which said, 'From dust you came, to dust you shall return.' I'd thought of that passage as talking about death. But it fit us now, too. 'From Earth mankind came, to Earth we must return,' I paraphrased. But were we returning to die, perhaps? I decided not to think too much about that.

None of us really knew what lay ahead down there, not even Darien. The briefing had made this all too clear. Earth was supposed to be the home of the true faith, the religion of the Lord of the Universe. Yet what would this religion be? Were we facing another deception, like all the other places we'd been? I shuddered at this thought.

"From Earth you came, to Earth you *must* return." The words came back into my mind with a new emphasis. 'Yes, we really have no choice but to go to Earth. If we want to find the truth, this is the place we must look, maybe the only place left to look.'

As these thoughts filled my mind, the shuttle began to vibrate as its engines started. Darien pushed the ejection button, and with a sharp hiss we were away from the Colassene ship, dropping into the gravitational field of Earth.

"MOUNTAINTOPS AND VALLEYS"

CHAPTER 1

PRELUDE

"Well, I think it's about time for a female point-of-view in this tale."

"So do I, Ginna, but that's my job!" insisted Martina Sullien

"Come on, Martina, you know that I'm within you, and you are somehow part of me. And right now I'm talking to myself, or something—I guess."

"Well, remember we live in parallel worlds, but right now we're in my world, so that means you're me. Your turn will come if we go to visit your world."

"I still don't understand what this really means, Martina."

Jon, the eldest in the group, reached over and patted her shoulder. This in itself was strange because Martina and

Ginna both felt his touch. "No one completely understands it—not even the quantum physicists who first postulated it. The more they explored the Universe, the more unexplained things they found."

"Like black holes?" asked Danny, Ginna Parker's younger brother.

Jon nodded. "And anti-matter."

"Dark matter, too," added Jael's voice.

"The Theory of Parallel Universes was one that came about as a result of these discoveries," said Jon. "Then, when the GAP was discovered, we found we could travel between some of them."

"But why do we sometimes have our own thoughts, even when we're 'within' someone else?"

"I'm not sure, Danny," Jon shrugged. "We're still exploring and learning about this."

"How come you get all the fun, Martina?" Ginna interrupted. "All I get to do is watch and listen. Am I supposed to learn something by being inside your mind?"

Jon looked at her with concern in his eyes.

"You know it's more than that," Martina replied. "You are 'within' me right now, so you get to really experience what I've been through. I hope it will help you in the long run."

"Okay, you're right. I _am_ feeling the same things that you do, maybe even more than I should. And I sort of feel at home 'inside' you now. When can we get on with your story, so I can keep living it?"

Jon frowned at this but said nothing.

"I thought you didn't like the idea of being 'inside' someone else," laughed Martina. "When Jon first proposed this Parallel Universe experiment, you were really hesitant. Remember?"

"Well, a girl can change her mind, can't she?"

"All right, we'll continue Martina's story soon," said Jon. "But first I need you to meet someone. We two aren't the only ones who need to tell our side of the story. To get this part told, we'll need to go back and forth through those 'blinds' a few times."

"You mean back and forth between our parallel worlds?"

"That's right, Ginna. So now, I need to take you and Danny back to your time and your own home to introduce you to someone."

***

Everything was dark around them suddenly. There weren't any stars in the sky. In fact, all they could see was snow swirling in the air around them.

Along with the cold wetness, Ginna felt a sudden desolation. She was just herself— alone again. In her heart, she knew Martina was gone, and it felt awful. 'I didn't know it would be like this,' she thought. 'I feel so empty without her. What do I do now?'

"Danny, where are you?" she screamed. She needed to

be with someone right now. This aloneness was wrenching her heart, which felt like it was already broken into many pieces.

"Right here, Ginna! Reach out your hand!"

She reached with both hands and, on her left, she felt her brother's arm. She grabbed quickly and held on tightly.

"Hey, don't squeeze so hard!"

"Oops! Sorry, Danny. I just don't want to lose you."

"Are we back in Colorado?"

"I can't see anything with all this snow, but it sure feels like an eastern Colorado snowstorm."

Danny was groping with his free hand in the air, trying to find something—anything—solid. Then, he felt the rough wood. "Hey, Ginna, I think I've found the porch rail."

"Where?"

"Here." He led her to the only solid thing he could feel and put her hand under his.

"Yeah! I think it *is* our back porch."

Carefully, so as not to lose their grip, the two children groped their way along the railing. Then Ginna felt her foot hit something.

"Ouch! There's a step, I think. I just hit it."

She guided Danny to where her foot struck. "Yes," he said. "These are the back steps."

At last, they worked their way onto the porch, through the creaking back door, and tumbled into the house.

"Gosh! I never thought I'd be so glad to see our old kitchen," she said.

"Me neither."

"Why did they bring us back in a blizzard?"

"I don't think they meant to, Ginna. Sometimes the time factor can be off. Jael told me."

"Where are they anyway? I thought Jon said he wanted us to meet someone."

"I wonder if they got lost in the blizzard, too."

Just then there came a crashing sound on the porch, and the back door flew open. Snow swirled into the kitchen, and along with it came Martina. Right behind her was a smaller girl with red hair.

"Whew!" she cried. "I'm really sorry about the snow. I'm new at this time-travel stuff."

"Martina!" Ginna grabbed her with a fierce grip.

"Watch it! Don't choke me, Ginna."

She released her grip, but still held onto Martina's arm. "I feel so empty without you."

"Hey, it's okay," came another familiar voice.

Ginna felt Jon's arm across her shoulders. She found herself leaning into him. "I feel like half my heart has been torn away, Jon."

"You'll be okay," he rubbed the palm of her hand with his thumb. This felt somehow familiar. It must be something he did with Martina often.

"I sure hope so," she sighed. She looked up at both

of them and realized with a start how strange it was to see Martina with her own eyes, instead of seeing things *through* Martina's eyes. 'Will I ever get to be inside her mind again?' she thought wistfully.

"I'm sorry about the crossing," Jon was saying. "I was putting too much stock in Ginna's being firstborn, and forgot how inexperienced she was."

Now Ginna looked at both of them in amazement. "You mean I have this GAP-crossing power, too?"

Jon nodded. "It would be better if you got some training in using it, though."

"I don't see how I can be here in the Twenty-first Century when it hasn't even been discovered yet," she sighed.

"That's true," he shrugged. "Anyway, when I realized there was a problem, I stepped into the GAP to help you." Jon took her hand. "I'm sorry."

For a moment, Martina looked angry, seeing Jon holding Ginna's hand, but she said, "Thanks, Honey." Then she turned to Danny and Ginna. "So, anyway, this is Raina."

"Hi, Raina," said Danny.

"She's Jason's sister from Terres."

"How did she escape the terrible fire and all?" Ginna asked.

"We're going to let her tell her whole story," Jon said.

Both of the children turned to Raina expectantly.

"You're welcome to sit on our old couch," said Ginna. "That seems to be where most of this GAP-crossing Time-Travel takes place."

Martina and Jon chuckled and followed Ginna into the tiny living room.

"When do I get to go back 'within' you, Martina?"

"Not for a while, Ginna. Raina needs to tell us her story. And I wasn't there for most of it."

Ginna let out a long sigh. "Okay, if we have to."

Jon was looking at her quizzically again, as though he was trying to decipher something in her face. Then he got out that strange fluted lamp they'd seen before.

"So, here we are again," he said. "Are you ready, Raina?"

"Yes, Jon."

The swirling colors from the lamp danced around the walls of the room. Ginna focused her eyes on Raina, though. 'She looks close to my age,' she thought. 'I hope her story can help me feel better about living in this place and time, a place that doesn't feel like home to me now.'

Raina's voice began with a sort of wordless chant, a different sound than they'd heard before. When she started to weave her story, the colors from the lamp became redder than ever before. Soon they found themselves in the middle of a raging inferno.

Thank you!

Thank you for joining me. If you liked the story and have a minute to spare, I would appreciate a short comment on the page or site where you bought the book.

Reviews from readers like you make a huge difference to helping new readers find stories similar to The Peaks series: *Searching for Maia.*

- Amazon
- Barnes & Noble
- Goodreads
- iBooks

Thank you!

M. F. Erler

ABOUT THE AUTHOR

M.F. Erler has been writing since she was about 14 years old. In fact, some of the initial ideas and characters for "The Peaks at the Edge of the World" were conceived when she was in high school, while writing assignments for freshman English class. Her lifelong goal has been to get the Peaks Trilogy out to readers, and thanks to new developments in electronic publishing, her dream has been fulfilled.

Fantasy and Science Fiction have long been among her favorite reading materials, and her favorite authors are C.S. Lewis and J.R.R. Tolkien. She is also interested in history, comparative religion, ecology, and music. Her previous publications include non-fiction articles in "Today's Christian Parent" and "Social Studies and the Young Learner." She has worked as an Environmental

Education teacher and facilitator, and also as a music teacher. Hobbies include reading, playing several musical instruments, and needlework.

She and her husband, Paul, have two adult children. All make their home in the Pacific Northwest.

Contact Frances at mferler@peaksandbeyond.com
Or follow her blog at PeaksAndBeyond.com